UNDER A CLOUD OF GUILT

"What's going on, Grandpa? I've never seen Daddy act like this."

Grandpa shook his head. "I reckon he's had a lot to worry about lately. This thing just hit him at the wrong time. Your Daddy's a proud man, John-Boy. But it's the kind of pride that sure wouldn't let him steal anything."

"But how come he didn't just tell Sheriff Bridges where he went that day?"

Grandpa shook his head, as baffled as John-Boy. "I reckon maybe it was partly the sheriff's fault. He got your Daddy's back up right from the start."

"But it sounded like he thought maybe there was a chance Daddy did take those goblets."

Grandpa nodded. "That's what I mean. But it'll work out, John-Boy."

The Waltons
THE EASTER STORY
Robert Weverka

Based on the television series
created by Earl Hamner, Jr.

RLI: VLM 5 (VLR 3–7)
IL 5–adult

THE WALTONS: THE EASTER STORY
A Bantam Book / February 1976
2nd printing

Published simultaneously in the United States and Canada

Bantam Books are published by Bantam Books, Inc. Its trade-
mark, consisting of the words "Bantam Books" and the por-
trayal of a bantam, is registered in the United States Patent
Office and in other countries. Marca Registrada. Bantam
Books, Inc., 666 Fifth Avenue, New York, New York 10019.

PRINTED IN THE UNITED STATES OF AMERICA

I

"Come on, John-Boy! Can't sleep all day!"

The voice seemed to come from miles away. After a single knock on the door, the footsteps faded away.

John-Boy opened his eyes for only a moment. On the table next to his bed he saw his pencil and writing pad. But they quickly faded away and he promptly returned to sleep.

"Time to get up, John-Boy."

This time it was his mother's voice, and her footsteps also continued down the hall.

John-Boy blinked at the table again. Then, almost reluctantly, the groggy world of sleep slowly dissolved. He rolled over, keeping the feather quilt tight around his neck, and gazed at the window. After a minute, he smiled.

It was a cold, dark, blustery morning. Gusts of wind were throwing bits of hail and snow against the window. But they were sporadic gusts. One minute everything was whirling and thrashing. Then, as quickly, it was all silence, with soft snowflakes drifting quietly down.

John-Boy loved this kind of weather. As long as the house was warm and cozy, it was like watching a great battle of the elements from a protected cocoon.

He finally rolled to his back and for several minutes enjoyed the luxuriant warmth of his bed. It was Sunday. From downstairs he could hear the voices and muffled laughter of the rest of the family, and he wondered if they would be going to church today.

1

He could remember going when there were deep snowdrifts, and during heavy rainstorms. But those were on special occasions like Christmas or Easter. As far as he knew, there was nothing unusual going on today. But he hoped they would go. He felt good—like this was a good day for going to church.

He slid quickly out of bed. The floor was icy, and even before taking off his pajamas he put on some wool socks. Then, shivering a little, he pulled on his pants and shirt, peering more intently out the window.

Off to the east the sky looked pale enough to suggest the storm would be passing quickly. Good, he thought. He laced on his heavy winter shoes and headed for the kitchen.

He was the last one down. Most of the family had already finished eating, and they had a guest for breakfast.

"Mornen, everybody. Hi, G. W."

"Mornen, John-Boy."

G. W. Haines was a gangly, freckled-faced boy, the same age as Mary Ellen. The two of them had been spending a great deal of time together lately, most of it throwing a baseball, trying to "burn" the other's hands with hard pitches. But this morning G. W. looked like he was dressed for church.

John-Boy warmed himself by the stove before he sat down.

"How late were you up last night, John-Boy?" his father asked.

"Oh, 'bout midnight, I reckon, Daddy." It had been well past one o'clock before John-Boy finally put his notebook aside. But he didn't think his mother would be too pleased to hear that.

"Don't see why people can't write stories in the daylight," Grandma commented.

John-Boy smiled. "Can't do that and chop wood at the same time, Grandma."

"Well, anyway," Grandpa said, apparently finishing up a story he'd been telling when John-Boy came in,

"Old Harvey, he just took the tires off that Stanley Steamer, drove it up on the railroad tracks and high-balled it into Richmond. Beat them other racen cars by twenty minutes—Barney Oldfield included."

The others laughed, but Ben was skeptical. "Is that really true, Grandpa?"

"Course it's true. You don't think I'd go maken up a story like that, do you?"

"But on a standard gauge railroad the tracks are four feet, eight and a half inches apart. I don't think the wheels of a Stanley Steamer would fit."

"I think he's got you there, Pa," John smiled.

Grandpa shook his head, unruffled. "People made do in those days, Ben. Not like today when everythen's conveniently worked out. Of course the wheels didn't fit. But Harvey done it anyway. You don't think I'd go maken up untrue stories when we got a guest in the house, do you? You believe it, don't you, G. W.?"

"Yes, sir."

"There you are, Ben. Pass me some more of them hotcakes, would you, Livvy?"

Ben frowned, but gave it up.

"We goen to church this mornen, Mama?" Mary Ellen asked.

"We'll see, dear. If the weather clears up."

"Be cleared up and the sun shinen in forty-five minutes," Grandpa said, "Gusten winds like this means the tail end of the storm."

"I think Grandpa's right," John-Boy agreed. "Clouds are breaken up in the east."

"Red sky in the mornen, sailor's warnen; red sky at night, sailor's delight."

"Nobody said anythen about a red sky, Grandpa."

"Didn't say they did. Just tryen to pass on a little learnen about the weather to you kids." Grandpa grinned and handed John-Boy the platter of hotcakes. "Afraid that's the last piece of bacon, John-Boy."

Olivia pushed her chair back. "I'll cook up some more."

"No, I'll do it," Grandma quickly said. "You just

finish your breakfast, daughter. No use in tiren yourself out any more."

"You ailin', Livvy?" John asked.

John-Boy, along with everyone else, looked closely at her. She did look tired.

"Now, don't everybody start maken a fuss. It's just a headache, and a touch of the usual winter rheumatism."

"And I say she's got a fever," Grandma said from the stove. "Feel her forehead, John."

John reached a hand across. "Well, maybe a little."

"My head's always warm," Olivia said.

"I say it's the grippe," Grandma went on, "Everybody's getten it. This damp weather seeps right through your bones."

Grandpa nodded. "I reckon we been lucky around here. Ike was tellen me Fanny Tatum's been in bed for a week. And all the Coverdales got it."

"Maybe you ought to lie down, Mama," Erin suggested.

"I can drive everybody to church," John-Boy offered.

Olivia shook her head. "Now, let's just drop the subject. If I'm getten the grippe, I don't reckon a short ride over to church is goen to make any difference one way or the other. And if I'm gonna be sick, I think I'd rather have the Lord on my side anyway."

As if in response to her statement, a shaft of sunlight suddenly broke through the kitchen window, brightening the room. "There you are," she smiled, "The Lord obviously agrees with me."

An hour later, when they started for church, the dark clouds had all passed far to the west. The sun was bright and clear, but it provided no comfort against the raw cold of the buffeting winds. Going out to the truck, the thin layer of snow crunched softly underfoot.

John drove, with Olivia and Grandma bundled up in the cab beside him, while all the others, including

G. W. Haines, huddled beneath heavy blankets in the back.

Their first stop would be the old Claybourne house—or Claybourne Hall, as the Claybourne family called it. There, they would leave John-Boy's father, and John-Boy would drive the rest of them on to church.

"You're goen to fix the Claybournes' refrigerator on a *Sunday*?" Grandma asked when John suggested they drop him off.

"We gotta eat on Sundays, Mama. If the Lord don't provide us enough food from my worken six days a week, I reckon He'll understand my worken on the seventh."

"The least you could do is go to church first and pay your respects. How about you, old man? You goen?"

Grandpa's church-going was sporadic, depending on his frame of mind. But whatever his decision, he always followed it through with determination and enthusiasm. He either stood his ground and flatly refused, or agreed to go and acted surprised that anyone should have asked him about it. This morning he chose the latter course. "Why I wouldn't miss it for the world, Esther!"

Through the next hour he sang hymns in a booming bass voice, and once they got settled and the blankets all arranged in the back of the truck, he thrust one hand out in the cold air and led everyone through three verses of "Rock of Ages."

John-Boy sang with the rest of them, but his thoughts drifted aimlessly. Except for the cold, it was a beautiful morning. To the north, the pine trees on the mountain looked like they'd all been dusted with powdered sugar. In the foothills and meadows below, the barren trees were spindly wrought-iron figures against the frozen earth.

"*Should my tears for ev-er flow,*" they all sang. "*Should my zeal no languor know.*"

John-Boy was relieved at how much better his

mother looked when they started for church. After breakfast and the sun came out, the color returned to her cheeks and she seemed to be more like herself. Her inspection of ears and hands and fingernails had been as rigorous as usual, and she had even spotted the baseball mitt Mary Ellen had tried to smuggle into the truck. This was promptly sent back to the house, and Mary Ellen informed that there would be no playing catch with G. W. after church.

"*Blest be the tie that binds,*" Grandpa sang, starting another hymn. "*Our hearts in Jesus' love: The fellowship of . . .*"

"Grandpa," Jason shouted from beneath the blanket, "We're goen to be all sung out before we even get to church."

"*. . . of Christian minds is like to that above,*" Grandpa boomed on.

John-Boy smiled, then grabbed for the railing as the truck swung sharply to the left and came to a stop.

"OK, John-Boy," his father said jumping out, "Hand me my toolbox there."

John-Boy got the toolbox and jumped down. "You sure you don't want us to pick you up after church, Daddy?"

"Nope. No tellen how long this'll take. And you watch out for that front tire, John-Boy."

"OK, Daddy." Almost all the tires on the truck were bad, but the one on the right front was down to the fabric.

"And take care of your mother. She starts ailen again, you just get her on home."

"I'm all right, John."

"Bye, Daddy."

After he banged the door shut, John watched them circle around and head back down the road.

"*Before our Father's throne,*" Grandpa's singing resumed. "*We pour united prayers.*"

As the voices faded John smiled and looked up at the Claybourne house. Aside from Judge Morley Baldwin's original place, which had been burned dur-

ing the Civil War, Claybourne Hall was unquestion-
ably the grandest home ever built in Jefferson
County.

It stood at the top of a broad, lawn-covered slope:
a huge mansion with stately white columns and gracious verandas. Even on this bitterly cold morning, it
wasn't hard to imagine the days when fancy carriages
filled its big driveway, and southern belles crowded
the verandas. But now, under the patches of snow, the
lawn looked like it hadn't been trimmed all winter.

John turned up his collar and headed up the broad
slope. The Claybournes were still about the richest
family in the county, he guessed. But like everyone
else, they had experienced their share of bad luck.
Carter Claybourne, who was only fifty-two years old,
had a heart attack and died about a year ago. So that
left only Mrs. Claybourne and the two kids—Stuart
Lee and Amelia.

Essentially, as far as Walton's Mountain was concerned, the Claybournes had always been a quiet
family. Carter Claybourne was said to have a variety
of financial interests, and spent most of his time in
Richmond or up in Baltimore. The family's social life
took place pretty much in the big cities, sometimes
taking them as far away as Atlanta and Birmingham.
So the Claybournes didn't mix a whole lot with the
farmers and working people of Walton's Mountain.
Still, they were always polite and friendly enough,
and on occasion Carter Claybourne had been very
generous with the other residents. None of the Claybournes ever attended the Baptist Church. But ten
years ago Carter Claybourne had surprised them with
a gift of two thousand dollars. And the three or four
times John had come out to repair an appliance or fix
drainpipes, Carter Claybourne had always handed him
a sealed envelope containing at least twice what he
normally would have charged.

Now, John presumed, twenty-one-year-old Stuart
Lee was the head of the family, and he guessed the
boy would be paying for the work he would do. He

wondered if Stuart Lee would be as generous as his
father. Considering how slow the woodcutting business had been lately, he certainly could use the
money.

Dewey Hamilton, the old Negro butler, answered
the door. Dewey had been with the Claybournes as
long as John could remember. But old age was catching up with him now, and he moved slowly.

"Mornen, Dewey, how you getten on?"

"Mornen, Mr. Walton. Come in, come in. We been
expecten you. I'm getten along tolerable, I reckon.
How's your family?"

"Fine, thank you."

The inside of the house always reminded John of a
museum. There was a heavy smell of floor wax and
furniture polish, and everyone always seemed to tip-
toe and talk in whispers. It was also chilly this morning.

Dewey led him past the big circular staircase and
down a long hallway. "This cold weather sure
enough aggravates a man's rheumatism, Mr. Walton.
Be glad when it's summertime again. Don't think this
old body o' mine can tolerate much more of this
blowin' and snowin'."

He moved across the kitchen shaking his head.
"Miz Docksteader, the cook, she's been gone a few
days, but right here's the refrigerator. Just stopped
hummen the day before she left, and there was no
more cold."

"I reckon with weather like this, a person don't
need a refrigerator much, Dewey."

"Ain't it the truth."

There was a soft *bong* and a red light flashed on a
wall panel.

"That'll be Miz Claybourne wanten her tea," Dewey
said. "If you'll excuse me, Mr. Walton."

John nodded and watched the old Negro pick up a
huge silver tray and hobble out the door.

Repairing refrigerators was not exactly John Walton's specialty. Washing machines, gasoline motors,

and most small electrical appliances were relatively
simple, and could be figured out with a little common
sense. But refrigerators with their compressors and
liquid coolants and thermostats could be tricky. After
an hour and a half, he found the trouble. It was simple enough. The automatic shut-off device controlled
by the thermostat had been shorted by a frayed wire
and the metal connector had melted completely apart.
John fashioned a new one by drilling holes in a piece
of scrap metal and bent it to fit the necessary con-
nections. Once it was in place he plugged in the cord
and smiled with satisfaction. The motor promptly
hummed into action.

"Hi, Mr. Walton."

Amelia Claybourne came bouncing into the kitchen
carrying a tray of empty breakfast things. She was a
pretty sixteen-year-old with long blonde hair and an
impish smile.

"Mornen, Amelia. How's it goen?" John worked
the refrigerator back into place.

"You get it fixed already?"

"Temporarily."

"Daddy never could fix anything. He'd just call
somebody in and have them do it."

"Well, I reckon your Daddy always had more important things to do."

"Yeah, I guess." She made a sour face. "Stuart Lee's
just like him."

John smiled and wiped his hands. "Well, like they
say, Amelia, 'Like father like son.'"

Mrs. Claybourne glided airily into the kitchen. She
was a handsome woman in her late forties, with ele-
gantly fixed hair. If John hadn't seen her before in the
same kind of gauzy gown, he would have guessed she
was dressed for a party. She greeted him and looked
sternly at her daughter.

"Amelia, darling, I hope you haven't been pestering
Mr. Walton."

"She's good company, Mrs. Claybourne. And the
fact is I'm all finished anyway."

She gave the refrigerator a look of surprise. "Now isn't that a miracle! Humming like brand-new. You're a wizard, Mr. Walton."

John smiled. "Don't see many of these electric refrigerators. They're a little more complicated than ice boxes."

"Amelia, go fetch your brother so he can settle accounts with Mr. Walton."

"OK."

"Darling, please don't slouch. Good posture is so important to a lady. And I find the term 'OK' quite unsuitable, dear."

"Bye, Mr. Walton."

It seemed to John that Amelia's posture was as good as any other teenaged girl's he'd ever seen. But she straightened into exaggerated stiffness as she left.

Mrs. Claybourne shook her head. "I'm afraid there is simply no hope for this new generation, Mr. Walton. In my day we took pride!"

John nodded and smiled to himself as he remembered the first time he ever saw Adelle Claybourne. It must have been twenty-five years ago when he was still a small boy, and the Claybournes were out riding in the first automobile he had ever seen. He was dazzled by the car. But he was even more impressed by the Claybournes' fancy clothes, and the proud way they sat on those high seats.

"Mrs. Claybourne, what I've done here is just temporary. There's a part inside that needs replacen."

"A part? Oh, dear."

"It's no problem. I can have one of Ike Godsey's suppliers pick it up over in Charlottesville." He smiled as Stuart Lee came in. "Mornen, Stuart Lee."

The young man was tall and slender, with an uncertain manner—as if not yet comfortable with his position as head of the family. He extended his hand with formality. "Mr. Walton."

Mrs. Claybourne moved toward the door. "It's always a pleasure to see you, Mr. Walton. Now, Stuart Lee, you be especially generous with our good neighbor. And please remember me to your lovely family, Mr. Walton."

"I'll do that, Mrs. Claybourne."

John gathered his tools and put them in the tool-box. "The temporary part I put in ought to hold fine until the new one comes, Stuart Lee. Then it'll only take a couple minutes to put it in."

"I see. I don't think I noticed your truck outside, Mr. Walton."

"No. The family brought me over on the way to church. I reckon I can walk home all right."

"I'll be happy to drive you. In fact I'm going right by your place."

"Well, I'd sure appreciate that, Stuart Lee. This box gets a little heavy sometimes."

The car Stuart Lee got out of the garage was a shiny Packard roadster. It was three or four years old now, but still about the nicest car John had ever ridden in. He especially appreciated the heater that was turning out fresh warm air as quickly as they reached the road.

"How you been getten along since your daddy passed on, Stuart Lee?"

"We—it's been difficult. Particularly for mother."

"Well, your daddy was a fine man. And I reckon your mama'll be all right in time. She's a strong lady."

Stuart Lee nodded, but didn't seem inclined to pursue the subject. They stopped by Ike Godsey's to order the refrigerator part, and then Stuart Lee drove in silence until they got to the house. He drew a sealed envelope from his jacket and handed it over. "Thank you very much, Mr. Walton."

"Thank *you*." John couldn't help smiling. Stuart Lee was handling the payment the same as his father had always done—as if counting out money was a distasteful act. The only difference was that his father usually invited John into his study for a taste of good bourbon before he gave him the envelope.

"You sure you don't want to come in and say hello? The family'd enjoy seein' you."

"No. The truth is, Mr. Walton, I'm on my way over to visit the Weatherbys."

John grinned. "Can't blame you for that. Blanche Weatherby's a handsome young lady. Give my best to her daddy."

"I'll do that, Mr. Walton."

"Say, Stuart Lee, as long as you're over there, I wouldn't mind your suggesten to Creighton Weatherby that I got some fine firewood for sale. Some good hard oak."

Stuart Lee didn't look too enthusiastic. "I wouldn't think it'd be worth your while to make deliveries that far."

"Be glad to. The way business is, I'll deliver it, stack it, and chop it into kindlin if he wants." John grinned. "In fact, if it'll help make a sale, you tell him I'll come over and light his fire every mornen and get his coffee goen."

Stuart Lee forced a smile and nodded impatiently.

"How about yourself?" John asked, "I reckon you've about used up that last load I brought you."

"No, I think we have enough for the present."

John nodded. "Well, you let me know. Much obliged for the ride."

John watched the roadster drive off and then headed for the sawmill. He felt a little sorry for Stuart Lee Claybourne. The boy seemed to have twenty things on his mind all at once, and wasn't able to cope with any of them. Maybe being rich didn't make life so easy after all.

"Daddy!"

John stopped short. There was a note of urgency in Ben's voice and he was flying across the back yard at full speed.

"Daddy, Mama's real sick! She fell down at church and we had to carry her up to bed!"

"What d'you mean she fell down?"

"It was like she fainted or something. She said her legs just gave out on her. And then it happened again when we got home. Grandpa and John-Boy had to carry her up the stairs."

It might be nothing serious—just the start of a bad case of the grippe. But Olivia generally wasn't hit hard by the usual sicknesses. John left his toolbox outside the door and went quickly into the kitchen.

Mary Ellen was at the stove, waiting for water to boil. "Grandma told me to make some tea."

At the table the other kids had worried looks. John took the stairs two at a time. He shouldn't have let her go to church, he told himself. In weather like this, the grippe could easily turn into pneumonia. And even Olivia wasn't strong enough to fight off something like that.

The door was open. Grandma and Grandpa were beside the bed, and John-Boy was curled forward in the corner chair.

"She's got a bad fever, John," Grandpa said.

"Strangest thing I ever saw," Grandma added.

John eased down on the edge of the bed and picked up her hand. Her eyes were closed, and he was startled by how drawn and weak she looked. This morning she was pale and looked a little tired. But now there was no doubt about her being sick. Her face glistened with mositure, and the deep red splotches left no doubt about the intensity of her fever. John touched her forehead and pushed aside a sticky strand of hair.

"Olivia?"

She didn't seem to hear him.

"How long has she been like this?"

"Just the last five minutes," Grandma said.

Grandpa shook his head. "She laughed about it when she fell down leaven the church. Said she must have tripped on somethen. Then it happened again comen in the house."

"We got her right to bed and she went to sleep. Then, just a few minutes ago she started shaken and the fever came on real bad."

"John-Boy, you'd better go for the doctor."

Grandpa rose. "I'll go with him."

"Daddy, that front tire is about flat. It was gotten low on the way home from church, but I didn't want to stop and change it."

John groaned inwardly. This was about the worst time in the world to get a flat. "Never mind, go anyway. There won't be any loss if you tear up that tire."

"What do you think Mama's got, Daddy?"

"I don't know. Just hurry, son."

The next hour and a half seemed like an eternity for John. After Mary Ellen brought up the tea. Olivia awakened for a couple minutes. But it was hard to say if she was really awake. She blinked uncertainly at John, and then smiled and pushed back her damp hair.

"I feel so silly. Did they tell you I fell down at church?"

"Yes, they did. You feel like havin' some tea?"

"I feel like I ought to be up gotten supper ready. Where's your ring, John?"

The question puzzled him until he realized she was holding his left hand, her fingers working over his.

"It's in my pocket. I take it off when I'm worken—so it won't get scratched." He smiled, but then looked more closely at her. She was looking at him, but her eyes were not focused.

"Are they comen for supper?" she asked.

John glanced across the bed. Grandma shrugged and shook her head.

"Who, sweetheart?"

"The Claybournes. I'd better get supper started if they're comen."

John wasn't sure how to respond. There was no question about her being delirious from the fever. She blinked again and closed her eyes.

"But my legs ache. I don't think I can get down the stairs." Her voice trailed off. "I do wish you'd wear your ring, John."

Her breathing became heavy again. She turned her head, gasping for breath, and was once more asleep.

While they waited, John alternated between sitting at her side and standing at the window. He was worried. He'd never seen Olivia quite so bad from any kind of a fever. On the other hand—as Grandma had said this morning—it could still be something as common as the grippe.

He smiled when he thought about her mentioning his ring. Standing at the window, he fished it from his pocket and slipped it back on his finger. There was nothing fancy about the ring. It was a heavy gold wedding band with no decorations. It had been his idea to get it in the first place. But now she never wanted him to take it off.

Dr. Vance was a tall slender man in his midforties, and his rimless glasses and stiff posture gave him a stern, businesslike manner. He had opened his office only two years ago—closer to Charlottesville than Walton's Mountain, and most of his patients came from the larger community. But since Dr. Shackleford had retired, there wasn't any choice for those in Walton's Mountain.

When he finally arrived he came directly up.

"You say she fell down twice?" he asked as he checked her pulse.

"Yes."

He nodded and got out his stethoscope. For several minutes he shifted the instrument around, listening to her heartbeat, but he said nothing. He put the stethoscope away and brought out a flashlight to look at her throat. When this was done, he gently worked his fingers under her chin, feeling her neck. In her feverish sleep, Olivia was oblivious to his probing.

Grandma finally rose and moved toward the door. "I think I'll go downstairs, John."

"All right, Mama."

John could tell nothing from the doctor's thoughtful frown. After he had finished with her neck he sat back in a chair and gazed at her through a full minute of silence. He finally rose and pulled off his jacket.

"Would you mind waiting outside for a couple minutes, Mr. Walton?"

"What do you think it is, Doc?"

The doctor shook his head. "I'm not sure."

Olivia had polio.

There was probably no way in the world for a doctor to make such an announcement in a gentle way. Nor can anyone ever be fully prepared to hear such news.

It took Dr. Vance ten more minutes to complete his examination. His suspicions were strong, and they were quickly confirmed. When he opened the door for John he smiled grimly and asked him to sit down. The doctor took the chair facing him and leaned forward, his voice as gentle as he could make it.

"I could be wrong, Mr. Walton. Sometimes these things are tricky and hard to diagnose. But in your wife's case, the symptoms are almost classic. She has the tremors, and the stiffness and pain in the neck and back. But even more significant is the flaccid paralysis of the voluntary muscles."

From the doctor's tone John Walton knew it was bad. "I don't think I understand," he said thickly.

"I'm afraid, Mr. Walton, that your wife has anterior poliomyelitis. It's more commonly known as polio. Infantile paralysis."

Polio. As far as John Walton knew there had only ever been one case of polio in Walton's Mountain. It was tragic—a little six-year-old girl who had been full of energy and laughter before it happened. He could remember her now; sitting in a wheelchair at the side of Miss Hunter's classroom. Her legs were no more than tiny stems—both heavily shackled in steel and leather. But mostly he remembered her eyes. They had the vacant, faraway look of suffering and hopeless, unattainable dreams. John closed his eyes for a minute, then looked over at Olivia.

"I'm sorry, Mr. Walton. I wish I had some doubts."

John nodded, his voice barely audible. "Shouldn't we take her to a hospital?"

"No. The strain really wouldn't be worth it. Complete rest is the best thing. I don't think she should leave her bed."

"I see."

"Are you all right, Mr. Walton?"

John took a deep breath and looked at the doctor. He nodded. "Yes, I'm all right."

"It's also very important that the children don't go near her. The disease is contagious."

"I understand."

After a minute the doctor rose and put his jacket back on.

"Doc—is there anything you can give her? Anything that'll help?"

The doctor sighed. "No. That's the terrible thing about polio. There's no known medicine that can help. We just have to hope the damage won't be too great. The disease spreads through the nervous system, eventually reaching the spinal cord or brain. If the cells are destroyed completely, it's impossible for them to regenerate."

John closed his eyes. What the doctor was saying was that she would be crippled. Why, he wondered. Why Olivia?

"Mr. Walton, I'm afraid there's nothing more I can do. I should be going."

John nodded.

"If you would like, I can—explain it to the rest of the family."

John looked at him, then shook his head. "No. No, I'd better do that."

"Yes, that's probably best. And maybe you'd better walk me out to the car."

John understood the request. If the doctor went out alone, everyone would want to question him. "Yes," he nodded. He finally pulled himself to his feet and went to the bed.

Olivia. Please, God, help her, he thought, please help her.

It was dark outside now. The ground was frozen and the stars were shining through a brittle black sky.

"I'm sorry, Mr. Walton. I'll be back again tomorrow. Just try to help her rest. And be sure the children don't go near her."

John nodded. The doctor started his car and the tires crunched softly away.

For several minutes he stood in numbed silence, looking off at the frosted silhouette of the mountain and the emptiness beyond. He wondered if there really was a God. And he wondered if in His scheme of things Olivia was destined for something like this. If that was so, this was the cruelest, most unjust world imaginable.

"Daddy?"

John-Boy's voice was soft and came from only a few feet behind him. John turned.

In the reflected light from the house, John-Boy could clearly see his father's face. He could see the despair, and the sagging shoulders, and the tears standing in his eyes. His father's voice was thick and barely audible.

"John-Boy, your mother has polio. Infantile paralysis."

John-Boy's mouth opened, but quickly closed, his throat clogged. Oh, my God, he thought. Oh, my God! The words kept repeating themselves in his head.

"It's gonna be hard on your grandpa and grandma, John-Boy. And worse for the kids. Until tomorrow I think we'd better just tell 'em she's got a bad fever and it will probably be down in the mornen." He took a deep, unsteady breath. "You and me'll have to help 'em face it. I'm gonna need your help, son."

John-Boy nodded, unable to speak.

His father looked off to the side. "If you feel like

stayen outside for awhile, go ahead. I reckon I'll be doen some cryen tonight myself."

John-Boy felt a hand on his shoulder. It slipped away and his father's heavy footsteps moved up the porch. When the door closed John-Boy clamped his eyes shut, trying to hold back the tears. "Mama," he said softly. He turned to the bannister post and buried his face in his arms.

II

The following day became a long, weary vigil—
waiting and hoping for some change in Olivia's condition. Through breakfast and going off to school,
John-Boy stoically answered the questions of his anxious brothers and sisters. They couldn't see their
mother, he told them, because she wasn't awake yet.
She needed all the sleep she could get. The doctor
had said nothing definite, but he was sure the fever
would go down sometime during the day. And yes, if
she was feeling better, they could see her when they
got home from school. He tried his best to sound
hopeful, but he doubted if he was very convincing.
Long before they reached school the questions ceased,
and they trudged on in grim silence.

John had told Grandma and Grandpa what the
doctor had said as quickly as he went back in the
house the previous night. He took them into their
own room and, using the same preparatory request as
the doctor, asked them to sit down.

How hard it had hit them, John couldn't be sure.
They were silent for a long moment. The tears slowly
formed in his mother's eyes. Then, with a thick voice,
Grandpa asked questions about Olivia's chances for
recovery, what they could do to help, and how certain the doctor was about his diagnosis. Grandma
didn't say a word. Her eyes drifted off to an empty
place on the wall, and then Grandpa told John they
would be out in a few minutes.

John had no illusions about the children's doubts.

But their fears, along with their wishful desires for their mother's recovery, prevented them from asking questions that might bring answers they didn't want to hear. After John-Boy led them off to school, Grandpa took care of cleaning up the kitchen, and John and Grandma returned to Olivia's side.

There had been no significant change. At times the flush disappeared from her face, and she seemed to awaken. She would smile and say she was feeling better, and request a drink of water, or ask what time it was. But then she would make some incongruous statement that indicated she was still only half conscious. Then her eyes dulled, the fever boiled, and once more she was in a gasping delirium.

Grandma bathed her face and cooled her neck and arms with a wet cloth, but there was nothing more she could do.

"John, there's no use in your hangen around here pacen the floor," she finally sighed, "You might as well go out and do some work. Get your mind off it."

"I don't think I could do any work, Mama."

"Well, go try. Or take a walk or somethen."

John left the room. But he didn't go directly downstairs. For no particular reason he went into each of the children's rooms and stood for several minutes. He looked at their toys and books, and at the odd little things that all children seem to collect. In each of them he saw part of Olivia. She had selected most of the toys and books. And she had remarked on each of the collected things; or suggested where it might be put; or tried to persuade them to get rid of it. And because of the children's anxiety over her illness, the beds were made extra neatly this morning, and everything was picked up.

"I think I'll go out and see about that bad tire, Pa," he said when he finally went down to the kitchen.

"Afraid there's not much left of it to see about."

"Well, I can put on the spare anyway."

"Want some help?"

"No. I think I can handle it."

Olivia had little recollection of the last twenty-four hours. At the church she knew there was something seriously wrong with her. At first, during Reverend Fordwick's sermon, there were waves of dizziness that prompted her to grab the edge of the pew, fearful that she was going to tumble forward onto the floor. As quickly as those left, her neck and back ached to the point of nausea. Once the service was concluded, she had hoped that standing up and walking would make her feel better. But on the front steps her legs had suddenly turned to unmanageable chunks of lead. She had grasped for Grandpa's arm, but that had only partially stopped her fall.

She hardly remembered going home in the truck. She had laughed, dismissing her fall at the church, telling them she must have tripped. But then the aches and nausea and dizziness came back. And even holding Grandpa's arm she couldn't make it to the back door of the house.

The pain was almost unbearable—a throbbing shaft that ran from the back of her head through her hips and past her knees. And then came the chills, followed by searing heat that drenched her with perspiration. On top of that, her throat had closed, making breathing almost impossible.

"Where's the pain, Mrs. Walton?"

The voice seemed to come from miles away. She smelled something sharp and pungent, and Dr. Vance was hovering close, holding something under her nose. In a hoarse, almost inaudible tone she told him about her neck and back. Then she felt his fingers brushing the side of her neck and examining her arms.

The rest consisted only of swirling glimpses of her room. She once saw John sitting in a chair next to the bed. But he was asleep. After that she was a twelve-year-old girl again. She was at a church picnic, competing in a footrace. She was far out in front when suddenly she fell. She laughed at the accident, but she couldn't get back on her feet. She lifted herself with her hands, but for some reason she couldn't draw her legs up beneath her. She shouted for help, and the other girls ran past, laughing, paying no attention to her.

There were other nightmares. She was in the delivery room of the Charlottesville hospital, and the pain was unbearable. She was screaming, but Dr. Shackleford was smiling down, quietly telling her she would have no trouble with the delivery because Jason was their second child. He didn't seem to hear her screams. And then Jason was standing beside the doctor, smiling, saying, "Don't worry, Mama."

Olivia knew these were crazy hallucinations caused by her high fever. But then another one would start and it seemed as real and terrifying as the last one. Her throat was sore and dry and seeing John beside her she asked for a glass of water. But before he could get it for her she was off somewhere else, transported by strange shapes and forms. Then she was gasping for breath, shivering, then suffocating from the heat.

It seemed to Olivia that this went on for days. Sometimes she awakened to see John or Grandma hovering over her, sponging off her forehead. Sometimes the room was empty. She would lie exhausted, trying to catch her breath for a minute. And then the room would slide away and once more she would be writhing and gasping in a swirl of confused images.

At last it seemed to be over. She was so tired she could not lift her head or arms, but the fever was gone. Grandma sat in a chair, half dozing, with a pot of tea beside her. The sun was shining crisply through the window and from out in the mill she could hear the muffled screech of John's saw. She sighed and turned her head.

"Mama?"

Grandma's head came up with a start and she gave her a questioning look. "Well! You feelen better?"

"I think the worst is over. Except I'm awfully tired."

Grandma looked relieved. She moved over and sat on the bed. "This tea's still warm. Think you could drink some?"

Olivia smiled and nodded.

Grandma propped her up with another pillow and poured the tea. "You want me to go get John?"

"No, don't bother him. I think I'll just go back to sleep in a minute." The tea tasted delicious. Grandma used sugar and milk and it seemed extra nourishing right now. Olivia smiled. "It's funny, my legs feel numb. I guess they're still asleep."

There was an odd look on Grandma's face. "Well, you just get all the rest you can."

"Was the doctor here?"

"Yes, and he'll be back this afternoon."

Olivia nodded. It seemed a useless expense having Dr. Vance come all the way out to the house. But right now she was too weary to question it. She put the empty cup aside and slid back under the covers. She could breathe easily now, and the warm tea was already making her drowsy. "I'm sorry to be all this trouble, Grandma."

She was asleep before she heard any response.

More than anything else, John dreaded telling the other children. Grandma and Grandpa, and even John-Boy, had seen enough of the world to know that disasters and tragedies were a part of life. But how did he tell the others? How could he explain a thing like this to children who had been told every Sunday that God rewarded people who were kind and generous and led good Christian lives? Nobody in the world was a better Christian than Olivia.

For a long time John sat on the back steps, staring off at nothing. The dog seemed to understand. His tail didn't wag, and his head rested heavily on John's leg. John finally gave him a sympathetic pat and pulled himself to his feet.

Grandpa was right about the front tire of the truck. There was nothing left of it to repair. John got out the jack and replaced the tire with the spare. He threw the shredded carcass into the back of the barn and came back to stare at the old truck.

He would be lucky if that spare or the other front tire lasted another twenty miles. But that might not matter. There wasn't much gas in the tank, and he had no money to buy anymore. Nor did he have any money for house paint, which he would be needing as quickly as spring came. Or money for new saw blades, or axes or wedges for splitting timbers. And now there would be doctor bills that were likely to go on for a long time.

John sometimes wondered if he hadn't been foolish trying to support his family all these years by cutting wood. Had he been selfish choosing an occupation that he enjoyed because he was independent—all to the detriment of his family? If he had gone down to Charlottesville years ago and gone to work at the soapstone quarry, would they be comfortable now, with plenty of money for the doctor, and maybe enough to send John-Boy to college? A lot of men had been laid off at the quarry, but there were plenty of them still there, still getting their weekly pay-checks.

John turned and moved slowly into the sawmill. It was a waste of time thinking about things like that. There was no chance of getting a job in Charlottes-ville now. And no matter how little woodcutting paid, he had to go on doing it.

He and Grandpa had spent the previous week hauling logs down from the mountain and stacking them at the side of the mill. George Halverson, a con-tractor in Charlottesville, had bid successfully on a contract for a new bridge on the Scottsville road, and John had agreed to supply the structural timbers at three dollars each. For the work involved, the job would not be very profitable. But the bridge was not scheduled to be built until late spring, so he'd figured on cutting the timbers during his spare time or on weekends. But right now he had no orders for firewood, nor anything else to do.

He put on his gloves, and with an angry heave, tumbled the top log down from the pile. Normally it took three of them to drag the big tree trunks over to the saw. But by twisting, swiveling, and wrestling one end and then the other, he managed to get it into position with an end raised to the saw table. Then he cranked up the motor, hoisted the other end of the log and guided it through.

With each successive cut the timber grew lighter. He trimmed it down, cut it smoothly to the precise rectangular measure, then sheared off the ends. Then he dragged the finished timber into the barn for storage.

He had wrestled the second log over and raised one end to the table when he saw John-Boy and the rest of the children coming. They were moving fast, with none of the usual straggling and horseplay. John turned off the saw motor and braced himself.

"How's Mama?" Mary Ellen asked, "Can we go see her, Daddy?"

John-Boy's level gaze indicated that he had told them nothing. In a way, John almost wished he had.

"I think you'd better wait until after the doctor comes. She's been sleepen most of the day."

"Is she feelen better?"

"A little."

"You need some help, Daddy?" John-Boy asked.

"No, I reckon I can handle this." He glanced off at the house and smiled. "But you can probably help your Grandpa with the ironen. He was out takin' clothes off the line a while back."

"I'll do it," Mary Ellen offered.

"And I'll start fixen supper," Erin added.

"And the rest of us can do some housecleanen," Jason said.

"Fine. Just try to keep it quiet."

John felt better as he watched them all hurry into

the house. Maybe they would be able to survive the bad news after all. On the other hand, he reflected, they might not be so enthusiastic when they found out those extra chores could become permanent duties.

John finished another timber before he shut down the saw for the day. Theoretically, that meant he had earned six dollars for his labors. But that didn't count cutting the trees and hauling them down from the mountain—nor the time it would take delivering them. And there would be no payment until May or June. Still, it gave him some satisfaction. At least he felt like he had earned a little credit on the future.

In the house everyone was at work, and John went on up to the bedroom. Grandma was smiling.

"Fever's all gone. She's been sleepen easy the past few hours."

John was relieved. He had no idea how the disease worked, but he assumed that the longer the fever lasted the more damage it was doing. He sat on the edge of the bed and took Olivia's hand. It was cool and dry now.

"Livvy?"

She stirred and took a long, easy breath.

"She had a cup of tea earlier."

John nodded. He gently stroked her hand and waited, and Grandma quietly turned on the lamp against the gathering darkness.

When Olivia's eyes opened, they were clear and bright once more, and she was smiling. "Hello, darling."

John grinned. No matter what the disease had done, it was still Olivia, and he still loved her very much.

"I think I've been sick."

"Yes, I think you have."

She looked at the ceiling and closed her eyes. She was still smiling, but the words came out hesitantly. "John—when I woke up earlier, I couldn't move my legs. I thought they were asleep—or that it was the fever. It isn't that, is it."

John swallowed hard and glanced uneasily at Grandma. "Olivia—"

"I still can't move them. They're numb. Does the doctor think I have polio?"

John stared at her, shocked by the almost casual tone of the question.

"Is it polio, John?"

"Yes," he finally managed, his voice almost inaudible.

She smiled tightly. "I thought it was." She gave him a sudden, anxious look. "The children. Are they all right? None of the children have gotten it, have they?"

"No, they're all fine, Livvy. Just worried about you."

She sighed with relief. "Thank heaven."

"Daddy?"

John-Boy's muffled voice came through the closed door. "Daddy, the doctor's here."

John rose and Olivia quickly brushed her hair back. Dr. Vance was there with his bag, and John-Boy moved discreetly off.

"Well, how's our patient getting along today?"

"Conscious," Olivia smiled. Grandma quickly propped her up with a pillow.

"That's certainly a step in the right direction."

Dr. Vance got out his stethoscope and held Olivia's wrist as he listened to her heartbeat. "Well, your heart still seems to be in the right place. How are you feeling?"

"Except for my legs, just fine. I'm not sure how they feel."

Dr. Vance seemed to catch his breath. He looked questioningly at John. John nodded.

"Well, it's good that you know, Mrs. Walton. And I'm glad to see you're facing it so calmly. Do you have any feeling at all below your waist?"

"No."

The doctor reached down and squeezed her toes, her ankle, and then the calf of her leg. "Feel that?"

"No."

He nodded. He got out a tongue depressor and had her open her mouth. That done, he checked her eyes.

Olivia took a long breath and gazed evenly at him. "Doctor, what's goen to happen?"

Dr. Vance was not comfortable with the question. He thought about it and pursed his lips. "For a long time, nothing. Mostly you're going to stay in bed and rest."

"I mean after that. Will I ever get any feelen back? Will I be able to walk?"

He evaded a direct answer. "That's hard to say, Mrs. Walton. People have recovered from polio. It depends on many things. In a day or two, if the feeling doesn't come back, I'll put some splints on your legs."

"Splints?" John asked.

"Yes. The theory is that the affected muscles are weak. That being the case, the healthy ones are likely to pull the weak ones out of shape—which causes crippling."

"How long will I have to wear the splints?"

Dr. Vance shook his head. "I've got to say it again: I just don't know."

Olivia stared at him and then looked away, bringing her hand to her forehead. She was in pain, John realized.

"You all right, Livvy?"

She made an effort to smile. "I just think I'd like to lay back again."

Both John and Grandma got the extra pillow out and eased her down. Dr. Vance watched grimly. "It'll probably be better if you don't sit up, Mrs. Walton. As I said, the important thing is not to tire yourself."

Olivia nodded and closed her eyes.

After he returned his stethoscope to his bag, Dr. Vance motioned his head toward the door. John followed him out to the hall.

"Considering her attitude, Mr. Walton, I think your wife is a very courageous person. This is good,

and can help her recovery. But it can also be dangerous. It's hard for anyone to believe they're really
going to lose the use of their arms or legs. Conse-
quently, they struggle to get them back to normal,
thinking their hard work will be rewarded. Unfortunately, in the case of polio, this is the worst thing
they can do. The struggling, or any kind of exercise,
is more likely to distort the muscles and limbs rather
than make them stronger. And that includes trying to
sit up. Do you understand what I mean?"

"That she should lie as still as she can?"

"Exactly. And I hope you can convince her of
that."

John nodded.

"Good," Dr. Vance smiled.

"Doctor?" John asked before he could go. "Can the
children come up now?"

Dr. Vance considered the question. "I think we'd
better be on the cautious side and wait another day."

"Is there any doubt about your diagnosis? I mean, is
it possible Olivia might have somethen else?"

He shook his head. "After what I've seen today,
there's no doubt whatsoever, Mr. Walton. I'm sorry."
He gave John a sympathetic pat on the arm. "I'll see
myself out."

John stood for awhile outside the closed door. He
heard the doctor's footsteps down the stairs, and then
the soft clunk of the front door closing. He finally
took a deep breath and headed for the stairs. There
was no point in putting it off now.

They seemed to know that it was coming, and that
it was bad news. John walked quietly into the kitchen
and sat down. Without a word they all moved to the
table. Mary Ellen brought him a cup of coffee, and he
looked at each of them as they sat down.

He had often wondered at the fact that he and
Olivia had produced such a diversity of children, and
that each in some way had his own talents, or
strength, or beauty. If anything should ever happen to

him, John suspected that John-Boy could rise to the occasion. As head of the family he could certainly do a better job than Stuart Lee Claybourne seemed to be doing. Jason, too, had those talents, and probably suffered only because he was the second child and had less opportunity now to develop them.

Ben seemed to live in a world of his own. For days on end he could be fascinated and completely absorbed with mathematical problems or schemes for making money. Mary Ellen; sometimes she seemed to have matured more than any of them. But, as often, she displayed the helplessness and confusions of her age. John suspected that Erin would take the news the hardest. Erin liked things to be neat and orderly, and she expected such virtues to be rewarded. As for Jim-Bob and Elizabeth, he wasn't sure they would completely understand what was happening. For them, the world was run by big people, and they had not yet begun to have questions about its contradictions.

John fervently wished he could tell them all that their mother was recovering from the grippe, or even pneumonia, and she would be down in the kitchen tomorrow morning inspecting their ears and sending them off to school.

"Your mother," he said, "is over the fever. She's resten a lot easier now. And she's feelen better."

There were no smiles or sighs of relief. They waited, staring at him, knowing from the tone of his voice that there was more.

"But she's been very sick. And—and she's goen to be sick for a long time. Your mother has a very serious disease. It's called polio." He broke off—not certain he could go on, or if it was necessary to go on.

There was not a sound. Elizabeth frowned, glancing at the others. Erin's mouth opened, but she quickly closed it, trembling as she stared at him.

John nodded. "It's not likely she'll ever be able to use her legs very much again. But how much she recovers depends a lot on us. We have to help her get as much rest as she can. And we have to help each other. Your mother will get better than she is right now. She'll be able to get around in a—in a wheelchair. Other than that, she'll still be the same. She'll be just like always. She'll still love you the way she always has."

Erin brought her hands to her face and turned away. The others sat stunned and silent.

"I've never even heard of polio," Elizabeth said bitterly.

"It's a disease that happens mostly to children," Jason said quietly.

Suddenly, for all of them, telling Elizabeth about the disease seemed a welcome distraction from their innermost thoughts.

"That little Marlowe girl had it," Mary Ellen said. "Remember?"

"The one with the crutches and wires on her legs?"

"That's right. She got it when she was four years old."

Elizabeth looked quickly at John for confirmation. He put his hand over hers and nodded. "Polio is a children's disease, sweetheart. But sometimes grownups have it too."

"Like President Roosevelt," John-Boy said.

"But—will Mama have to use crutches and have wires on her legs?"

"Well, it's really too soon for the doctor to tell about that."

"Daddy?" Jim-Bob asked, "You mean Mama won't ever be able to walk again?"

"Jim-Bob," Grandpa said, "A lot worse things can happen to people. And a lot of people have polio and do just fine. Look at Franklin Delano Roosevelt. He had polio when he was just about your mama's age. Hasn't stopped him none."

"Not so's you'd notice," John-Boy smiled.

They all smiled. But John knew their efforts to make the best of it were artificial. Once they had time to sift through their thoughts the full import of things would come crashing down on all of them.

"Daddy?" Elizabeth finally asked, "Why did it happen to Mama?"

It was the question John dreaded the most, and he still had no answer for it. He shook his head. "To tell you the truth, I'm havin' a little trouble understanden it myself."

"God works in mysterious ways," Grandpa said.

The statement brought no satisfaction to anyone at the table. They looked at him, but turned glumly away.

"Well," he said and pushed his chair back, "Come on, everybody. Time we got all these chores finished up."

Grandma came down and took some supper up for Olivia. The others ate in silence, each struggling with his own despairing thoughts. After the dishes were cleaned up, the children did homework and filed quietly upstairs. John turned off the last of the lights and found Olivia awake. He sat on the bed and smiled. "Feelen better?"

She nodded. "It felt good to eat somethen." She yawned sleepily and took his hand. "Did you get the Claybournes' refrigerator fixed? It's funny—that's about the last thing I remember. It seems like months ago."

"I got it runnen. But I have to go back and put in a new part."

"Did they pay you?"

She asked the question drowsily, but it jarred John's memory. He'd completely forgotten about the envelope Stuart Lee had handed him in the car. He had shoved it into his jacket pocket, and his jacket was over on the chair by the desk.

"Yes, Stuart Lee paid me."

"That's good," Olivia said, and she was suddenly sleeping again.

John rose and quietly crossed the room. That envelope could mean a couple used tires for the truck. And if Stuart Lee was as generous as his father had always been, there might even be some money left over. John found the envelope. He sat down at the desk and quickly slit it open. Then he blinked with disbelief.

It contained a single dollar bill.

John almost laughed. Stuart Lee couldn't be serious. Mrs. Claybourne had distinctly told him to be generous with "our good neighbor."

John sat back and stared at the creased and dirty bill. Was it possible Stuart Lee intended to pay him more when he returned to install the new part? He doubted it. Stuart Lee already had the envelope in his pocket when John told him he would have to come back.

No, John concluded. The dollar was probably all Stuart Lee intended to pay him. He sighed wearily and tossed the crumpled bill on the desk.

Erin took it the hardest, John-Boy wrote in his notebook. *I think Mary Ellen suspected the worst all along, while Jason, Ben, and Jim-Bob did their best to follow Daddy's example. At least outwardly, they accepted it as a tragedy that must be faced and dealt with. In Elizabeth's case, I'm not sure she fully understands yet. At her age I guess it's all just too mysterious and confusing.*

But Erin, I think, was shattered by the news. Erin believes everything in the world should be clean and pretty, and healthy and beautiful. For her, Mama has always been the perfect example of this. Tonight, when we all went to the bedroom door and wished Mama goodnight, Erin could hardly bring herself to speak.

For Mama's sake, I hope she'll . . .

"John-Boy?"

John-Boy closed his notebook and found Jason, Ben, and Jim-Bob at the door, all in their pajamas. They came in and sat on the bed.

"John-Boy, we were kind of thinken—about Mama and everythen. And, well—do you think Dr. Vance is a good doctor for Mama? I mean we think he probably knows everythen about measles and colds and broken arms, and that kind of stuff. But what Mama has is somethen kind of special, and maybe some other doctors know more about it."

"Like some doctors know about heart troubles," Ben added.

"When G. W. Haines broke his foot that time," Jim-Bob said, "his Daddy took him all the way down to Richmond to see some kind of a special bone doctor."

John-Boy nodded. It was a question that hadn't occurred to him. And probably not to his father. "I don't know. I reckon there isn't anybody who knows a whole lot about polio. At least that's what Dr. Vance told Daddy."

"But we could try, John-Boy. There might be some doctor in Charlottesville or Richmond who knows more than Dr. Vance. Maybe Daddy could go get 'em and bring 'em up here—at least to look at Mama."

John-Boy knew it wouldn't be as easy as that. Doctors who were specialists were probably very busy—and very expensive. His father already had money problems. "I don't know," he said again. "If there were any medicine or treatment for people with polio, I reckon Dr. Vance would have heard about it."

Their disappointment made John-Boy wish he hadn't sounded so negative. "But I guess it's somethen we ought to think about."

"Maybe we could ask G. W. where his Daddy took him," Jim-Bob suggested.

John-Boy nodded and changed the subject. "How's Erin and the girls takin' everythen?"

Jason shook his head. "Erin's been cryen ever since she went to bed."

"She doesn't even want to see Mama tomorrow."

"Why not?"

"She's afraid Mama's gonna be all twisted and ugly and in pain."

John-Boy winced at the description. When he brought the doctor up earlier this evening he had only glimpsed his mother. But she certainly hadn't looked that bad.

"And Elizabeth is sucking her thumb again," Ben said. "Mary Ellen screamed at us and told us to get out of their room."

"What were you doen in their room?"

Ben shrugged and they all gazed despairingly at him. My God, John-Boy thought—that's all they needed around the house right now: the kids all fighting or crying, and Elizabeth sucking her thumb again. It had been years since she did that. "Are they asleep?"

"No. Not when we left."

"Listen," John-Boy said, "Mama's bein' sick isn't goen to be the end of the world for us. She's still goen to be here, and she's still goen to be the same person she always was. But she's gonna need help from all of us. And Daddy and Grandma and Grandpa are gonna need help too. So let's not make the problem worse. Let's help 'em."

John-Boy wasn't sure if he impressed them with the urgency of the matter. But they all nodded.

"We'll help, John-Boy."

"Then you'd better go get some sleep. And I'll talk to the girls."

John-Boy waited until they were back in their bedroom, then knocked lightly and opened the girl's door. "Mary Ellen? Can I come in?"

He could hear Erin's muffled sobbing. Elizabeth seemed to be curled into a tiny ball, and Mary Ellen was lying on her back, staring at the ceiling. She glanced over, but said nothing. John-Boy closed the door and eased down on the edge of Erin's bed.

"I saw Mama today. Just for a minute, from the door."

Erin's sobbing stopped. She seemed to be holding her breath, scared to death of what was coming next.

"She looked fine. She hardly looked sick at all." He

gave her a minute to absorb this. "She was just sitten there, propped up in bed, smilen—talken to Grandma."

Erin turned over and stared hard at him. Her face was streaked with tears.

John-Boy smiled. "I reckon when someone gets real sick we expect 'em to look different, or be a different person. But the only thing different about Mama will be her legs. At least for a while she won't be able to walk."

Erin clamped her eyes shut. "She'll never be able to walk."

"Well, that might be, Erin. But the important things won't be changed—things like how she feels about us, and how we feel about her. And I reckon it's important to her that we don't change. I guess about the most valuable thing she has is our love for her. If we don't keep given' it to her, I reckon that'll be a lot worse for her than not bein' able to walk."

Erin gazed silently at him for a long time. Then the tears suddenly flooded back and she turned quickly away. "Oh, John-Boy, I'm so ashamed."

John-Boy put his hand on her shoulder and let her cry for a minute. "No cause to be ashamed. It's natural wanten people we care about to stay the same." He shook her gently. "Come on, Erin. We're all of us mixed up and scared. It's gonna be better tomorrow. We're goen to do the best we can, and we're goen to show Mama how much we really love her."

Erin nodded and sniffled back the tears.

Mary Ellen and Elizabeth had both turned to listen. Elizabeth took her thumb from her mouth and buried it deep under the covers. John-Boy smiled at her and moved toward the door.

"Now let's all get some sleep."

"John-Boy?" Mary Ellen murmured.

He paused at the door.

"Thanks," she said.

III

Their first visit with their mother had all the characteristics of a homecoming party. Through the afternoon, all seven of them impatiently watched the clock on the classroom wall. When Miss Hunter finally dismissed them they bolted for the door and headed home at a half run.

At the house Grandma helped Olivia change into her prettiest nightgown and then cleaned up the room while Olivia brushed her hair. Following Grandma's instructions, Grandpa made sugar cookies and a pitcher of lemonade while John washed the bedroom windows. When the thunder of footsteps hit the back porch and roared up the stairs, Olivia was ready and waiting.

They each got a hug and a kiss and a beaming smile. Then they sat on the floor or at the foot of the bed and Grandpa served the refreshments. If anything, it seemed that Olivia was more lighthearted than they had ever seen her. Elizabeth said she was going to learn to cook, and Jim-Bob said he already had plans to enlarge her vegetable garden. Olivia laughed and said that maybe she should have gotten sick a long time ago.

There were no longer any doubts or fears. Olivia was still their mother, and she was as warm and loving, and as dependably strong as ever.

After forty-five minutes John rose and shooed everyone out with a grin. If they all had such wonderful plans, he said, they'd better get started with them before they wore themselves out talking. And they had chores and homework to do before suppertime.

In the days that followed, John-Boy didn't at first fully appreciate what his mother was doing. But it soon became clear that she was going to permit no one to waste time brooding, or feeling sorry for her. And she was going to insure against it by encouraging each of them to think about and plan their own futures.

Before they all went off to school each day, they gathered in her bedroom. Smiling cheerfully, she asked each about his studies, or his homework, or their classmates. Sometimes she gently admonished them to apply themselves more, and to their inquiries about how she was feeling, she laughed and observed that it wasn't fair for everyone to be working so hard while she lolled around in bed all day.

When they arrived home from school she was in the same cheerful mood, and talked to them individually.

"John-Boy, I hope you've been given some thought to what you're goen to be taken in college next year. You'll be graduaten pretty soon, and you should be prepared. I been thinken about it all afternoon, picturen you on campus."

Even before his mother's illness John-Boy had grave doubts about ever going to college. Now, with all the medical expenses, it seemed like his chances were even more remote. He smiled. "You mean in my porkpie hat and raccoon coat?"

"No. What you wear doesn't concern me as much as what you'll be learnen—what classes you'll take."

"I'm not sure, Mama. And I reckon it's pretty hard to pass the entrance exams anyway."

"You know very well you can pass those exams, John-Boy. You just start thinken about what courses you're goen to take."

It was almost like a game, as if they were pretending she wasn't sick at all, and there was plenty of money. Still, in spite of his doubts, the conversation lifted John-Boy's spirits.

"I'll tell you what I'll do, Mama. It's only about twenty-five miles over to the campus. Suppose I drive over and get a catalogue. Then you and I can plot it all out."

"I think that's a wonderful idea." She smiled and gave him a questioning look. "Do you think I'm bein foolish?"

"No, I don't."

Whether his mother's encouragement was foolish or not, it had a dramatic effect on everyone in the family. Jason began practicing his guitar every spare minute he could find. There was going to be an amateur talent contest in Charlottesville, and Olivia convinced him he had a good chance of winning it. Ben sent off a letter to a magazine distributing company asking to be their salesman in the area—something he'd been talking about for almost a year. And Mary Ellen, who had turned down half a dozen invitations to school dances—mostly from G. W. Haines—because she didn't have any party dresses, was suddenly studying dress patterns and following Grandma all over the house with questions about sewing.

The biggest change came in Erin. Instead of shrinking from Olivia's illness and its possible consequences, she plunged headlong into the task of being the chief nurse of the household. Without being asked she took over the responsibilities of bed changing, giving Olivia baths, and propping her up in bed for visitors.

But for all Olivia's efforts, it was still impossible for her to disguise the pain she was suffering. In midsentence she might catch her breath and clamp her mouth shut for an instant. As quickly as the pain passed she would smile and brush it off. "No, no, it's nothing. I'm all right," she would respond to alarmed inquiries.

John was more aware of it than the others. Almost every night he was awakened by her gasping and painful efforts to turn herself over in the bed. And in the mornings it took her half an hour to gather enough strength to present a cheerful face to the children.

John protested only mildly when she began making efforts to sit up by herself. Dr. Vance had warned against it. But Olivia claimed she felt far worse, and experienced more pain when she lay flat on her back all day.

The first of what she called her exercises consisted only of getting an elbow and then a hand behind her to give her enough leverage to lift her head and shoulders. Then, with this accomplished, she began the task of swinging her head and rocking her upper body enough to get herself into an upright position. As often as not it would result in her falling to the side, or suddenly collapsing back to the pillow in pain.

When Dr. Vance arrived with the splints for her legs, Olivia lay in glum silence while he adjusted and secured them in place.

"You must realize, Mrs. Walton, that these are not supports for walking or moving around. They're simply protective devices. You still must not make any effort to move your legs or exert yourself in any way. Now, how do they feel? They don't hurt, do they?"

"No," she said, "I can't even feel them."

"That's fine."

Olivia twisted her head to look at them. "I just hope they don't interfere with my exercises."

The doctor smiled. "Well, it'll be a long time before you start doing any exercises. In the future we'll think about fitting you for braces. Then maybe we can work out some exercises to strengthen your arms."

"I've already been doen it. I can almost sit up by myself."

Dr. Vance glanced sharply at John, but turned quickly back as Olivia suddenly rocked to the side and got an elbow beneath her. She tried to get the other arm behind and swing up in one movement, but her hand slipped and she fell back. She laughed. "Well, I can almost get halfway up."

Dr. Vance was shocked. "Mrs. Walton, you really shouldn't do that."

"Why not?"

"Well, you may not be aware of it, but even in trying to sit up like that you tend to use your leg muscles. That's exactly what I'm cautioning you against doing."

"But I can't just lie here all day doen nothen."

Dr. Vance sighed with frustration and looked over at John. But John could only shake his head. Olivia had decided to exercise, and once she had made the decision, nothing short of tying her down to the bed was going to stop her.

"Mrs. Walton, if you hope to prevent your leg muscles from being distorted, that's exactly what you must do—lie there all day doing nothing."

"But Dr. Vance, you say that I won't ever walk again anyway. So what difference does it make if my leg muscles are distorted? In the meantime, I can't see any reason not to strengthen the muscles I can use."

Her logic was too much for him. He stared silently at her for a minute and finally nodded. "Well—you may have a point. But I'll warn you, it's not going to be as easy as you think."

Olivia smiled. "Now, the next question is, after I can sit up, how do I go about getten the feelen back in my legs?"

"Mrs. Walton, you should understand that with polio the nerves are destroyed. Now, skin or muscle, and even to some extent, bone tissue can regenerate itself. This is not the case with nerve tissue."

"What if they haven't been destroyed?"

"Well, that—yes, it's true that in some cases the nerves are only partially affected. However, that is rare."

"But let's assume I'm one of the rare cases. Then what should I do?"

Again Dr. Vance looked at John as if for help.

"Is there some kind of medicine?" John asked, "Somethen that would help?"

Dr. Vance shook his head. "Not that I know of." He sighed and got his bag. "I don't think either of you should get your hopes up too much. The recovery rate from polio is extremely low." He looked at Olivia and smiled grimly. "But I do admire your determination, Mrs. Walton. If those splints give you any discomfort let me know and I'll make some adjustments."

John walked him out to his car. "At least try to stop her from overdoing it, Mr. Walton. I've never heard of a patient behaving this way. Usually they're so exhausted from the ordeal it takes weeks before they can even lift their heads."

"Well, Olivia's kind of an unusual person."

Dr. Vance tossed his bag in the car. "I just hope she doesn't regret it later." He got in the car and John closed the door for him.

"Doc, I reckon we're runnen up quite a bill for your services. But I guess I'm in about the same spot as everybody else in Walton's Mountain. If I can pay a little bit each month, I'd sure appreciate it."

The doctor gave him a thin smile. "That'll be fine, Mr. Walton. However, considering your wife's behavior, I wonder if I'm not just wasting my time coming out here."

"Oh, she appreciates it, Doc. It's just that Olivia's not used to lying in bed much."

The doctor gave him a weary nod. "Well, I'll be back in a day or two."

John watched him drive off and then looked up at the bedroom window. According to what Dr. Vance said, even if he had a million dollars there was nothing more he could do for Olivia. That was the frustrating part of the whole thing. And as it was, he didn't even have enough to pay Dr. Vance to come out and check Olivia's pulse.

John shoved his hands in his back pockets and wandered over to the truck. For several minutes he gazed ruefully at the two front tires. It was hard to believe they were still holding air. Two layers of fabric were visible on the left one, and there was a distinct bulge at one spot. The tire on the right side didn't look much better.

The truck was loaded with firewood. In the past two days John had made a complete circuit of the valley, offering the two cords of wood at the price he usually charged for one. But no one had been even remotely interested. Most people had no cash at all, and were too deeply in debt to think about buying anything more on credit. Others had taken to cutting wood themselves to save what little money they had.

John looked over at his saw, and the big log he had dragged into place to cut into a timber for Halverson, the contractor. He wondered. If anyone in Jefferson County had any money, it was likely to be George Halverson. At least he had a going construction business. It was a chance. John took one last look at the tires, then started up the truck and headed for Ike Godsey's.

At least the weather had taken a turn for the better. The temperature at night still dropped below freezing, and patches of old snow remained in the chilly shadows of the trees. But the sun was pleasantly warm in the clear blue sky. With the truck so heavily loaded, John drove cautiously, avoiding the worst of the deep ruts and potholes.

The iron wood stove was going in Ike's store, giving the place a cozy warmth to go along with the smell of leather and sawdust and ground coffee.

"Hey, John! How you getten along?'

"Pretty good, Ike. How you doen?"

Ike was in the back, playing pool with Sheriff Ep Bridges.

"John, I'm real sorry to hear about Livvy," Ep said. "How's she feelen?"

"A lot better'n the doctor thinks she should, I reckon. He put some splints on her legs today."

Ike shook his head. "It's a real shame. Now there's Olivia, about as healthy as anybody you ever saw, and just struck down like that. Don't make no sense at all. How are the kids takin' it?"

"Real good, Ike. They're all pitchen in, maken the best of it."

"Well, you let us know if there's anythen we can do to help," Ep offered. "They don't make 'em any better'n Livvy."

"Thanks, Ep."

John watched while Ike carefully lined up an easy corner shot. He missed the ball entirely.

Ep Bridges laughed and moved around the table. "Ike, if you can't do no better'n that I'm goen to start shooten left-handed to make this a contest."

Ike massaged his elbow. "Got a little touch of the rheumatism this mornen."

John smiled. "Ike, you mind if I use your phone?"

"No, go right ahead."

John cranked the instrument and answered all of Fanny Tatum's questions about Olivia before he asked her to connect him with the Halverson Construction Company in Charlottesville.

"Olivia's got a big surprise comen pretty soon," Fanny said while she placed the call.

"Oh, what's that?"

"Well, I really shouldn't tell you, but the ladies at the church are maken her a big signature quilt. And John, it's just the most beautiful thing you ever saw."

"She'll sure like that."

"Don't you go tellen her now. I reckon it'll be ready tomorrow or the next day."

"I won't, Fanny."

A girl answered the phone and put John through to George Halverson.

"John, I wish you had a telephone up there so I could call you. I just can't tell you how bad I feel about Livvy. How's she getten along?"

John was surprised the news had traveled so fast.

But polio probably frightened people enough that word spread quickly.

"Doctor says she's doen better than expected, George. I'll tell her you asked."

"You be sure and do that. And how are you and the family getten on?"

John smiled. "Well, that's kind of why I called you, George. I've been worken on those timbers for that bridge job you've got comen up. I was wonderen if you might be able to take some a little early."

Halverson hesitated. "How early you mean, John? If you've got a problem storen 'em, I could probably put some in my equipment shed." He paused. "But I don't reckon that's what you're getten at, is it."

"No. I was hopen you might be able to pay for 'em early, too."

John heard the squeak of Halverson's chair tilting back, and he suddenly wished he hadn't asked. He hated the idea of accepting any kind of charity, or begging money from anyone. He forced a smile into his voice.

"Listen, it's not real urgent, George. Those things are just starten to pile up in my barn, and I thought if you wanted to take delivery early I just happen to have the time right now."

"John, I wish I could accommodate you. The fact is, I been over at the bank all mornen tryen to negotiate a loan, and they turned me down. I'm not sure I can meet my payroll this week. I sure wish that bridge job was starten tomorrow."

John dropped the subject. They talked about deer hunting for a few minutes and ended the conversation with John promising to come down and see him when he got the chance. He stood at the phone for a minute and looked back at the pool players.

"Hey, Ike. You or Ep got any need for some good oak firewood? Half price today."

"Not me," Ep said. "I got tired of haulen wood into the house and haulen ashes out. Got me one of them new oil stoves."

"Sorry, John," Ike added, "I think I got enough to last the rest of the winter. Oh, by the way, that refrigerator part you ordered for the Claybournes came in this mornen. It's right there by the cash register."

John took the part and got back into his truck. He might as well take the thing out and install it. And today was as good a time as any to have a little talk with Stuart Lee about the facts of life.

Driving out to the Claybournes, John thought about young Stuart Lee and wondered what the boy might have been thinking when he put the one dollar bill into that envelope. He'd probably never earned a penny in his life by working. And he probably had no idea what it cost to buy food and clothing for a family of eleven people—nor any idea what it would have cost him to have someone come up from Charlottesville to repair that refrigerator. Stuart Lee's father had bought him that new Packard roadster and sent him off to the University of Virginia, and no doubt kept his pockets full of spending money for four years. It wasn't too surprising if the boy had no understanding about money.

John cautioned himself against getting too angry about the whole thing. Very likely when the matter was brought to his attention, Stuart Lee would be embarrassed and pull out his wallet with all kinds of apologies.

For an instant, John thought somebody was deer hunting in the area. The loud bang seemed to come from his left, startlingly close. But then there was the sharp screech of air escaping from a tire and he was suddenly fighting the steering wheel, struggling to keep the heavy load from tilting too far to the side.

"Damn!' he said when he brought the truck to a stop.

It took him almost an hour to repair it. He had a patch kit and an old tire-boot under the front seat, but he had to use three patches to cover the three-inch slit in the innertube. And then his rusty old pump leaked more air than it forced into the tube.

Once he got the truck started again, John had grave doubts about how much longer either of the tires would last. But if he could get three more dollars from Stuart Lee he could probably make it down to Charlottesville and buy a couple used ones.

John parked in the back, and Dewey was at the door as quickly as he got his toolbox out. "Afternoon, Mr. Walton. Fine day, ain't it?"

"Sure is, Dewey. Your rheumatism feelen better?"

Dewey had a silver platter in his hand, polishing it. "Gone away completely, Mr. Walton. Feelen fine now. How's Mrs. Walton getten along?"

"Good as can be expected, I reckon. You got some place I can wash up before I get started here?"

Dewey showed him to a small washroom off the pantry, and John scrubbed the grease and dirt from his hands. When he came out, Mrs. Claybourne was leaving the kitchen. She smiled. "Oh, Mr. Walton. Dewey told me you were here. Would you care to have a cup of coffee with me in the drawing room?"

"I'd appreciate that, Mrs. Claybourne, but I reckon I'd better get that part into your refrigerator."

"Oh, I'm sure that can wait. And I do want to hear how Olivia's getting along. I was shocked to hear about it, Mr. Walton." She gave him a sympathetic smile. "I asked Dewey to serve coffee instead of tea. I know how you men prefer it."

John smiled. "Well, in that case—"

It had been years since John had been in the Claybournes' drawing room. That visit had been brief; only long enough to replace a pane of broken glass. It was an impressive room. One end was dominated by a white marble fireplace. Above it there was a huge oil painting of General Harlan McKelvey, Mrs. Claybourne's grandfather. There were smaller portraits along the side wall, and all the brightly polished furniture stood on yellow carpeting that felt as soft as a down comforter. Mrs. Claybourne led them across to the two sofas in front of the fireplace.

"I'd forgotten how grand this room is, Mrs. Claybourne. I don't think I've ever seen a room as pretty as this even in a magazine."

"Yes, this room is my sanctuary." She glanced around. "I always feel so much more secure surrounded by reminders of the past."

John smiled. "I know. There's the ruins of an old cabin up on the mountain that gives me the same feelen. Course it never was quite like this."

Dewey brought in a silver tray with coffee and cups, along with some pastries.

"Now, tell me about Olivia," Mrs. Claybourne said once they were served.

John told her what the doctor said and about Olivia's determination to bring some life back into her legs.

"Well, I hope she doesn't get her hopes up too high," Mrs. Claybourne commented. "Carter's second cousin in Savannah got polio when she was fourteen years old and she's never walked a step since, poor thing—and with the finest medical advice in the world. And the cost was appalling. I do hope the expense is not going to be too much of a problem for you."

John was tempted to bring up the question of Stuart Lee's payment for his repair services. But Mrs. Claybourne probably had less understanding about money than the boy did. "Oh, I reckon we'll get through it somehow, Mrs. Claybourne. Stuart Lee doesn't happen to be home today, does he?"

She smiled. "No. And I imagine you can guess where he is."

"The Weatherbys'?"

"I do think he's going to marry that girl." She sighed. "And Amelia—nearly sixteen—off to college in another year. It's really distressing to think about one's children growing up and gallivanting around the world. But you must know all about that, Mr. Walton."

"Yes, I do."

She frowned. "Stuart Lee did pay you the other day, didn't he?"

John hesitated. If he was going to bring up the subject, now was certainly the time. But it only seemed fair to confront Stuart Lee first. He smiled. "Yes, he did."

"Oh, good. Stuart Lee told me it was all taken care of. But he's been so distracted lately I thought he might have forgotten. I'm so glad he's learning about money and financial matters. With so many people doing without these days, I think it's in rather poor taste for us to indulge in any extravagances. Don't you, Mr. Walton?"

"Yes, m'am." He wondered if Stuart Lee might have regarded paying a decent wage to someone as an extravagance. John emptied his cup and returned it to the tray.

"Oh, do have one of these cream puffs, Mr. Walton. Stuart Lee gets them for me in Richmond."

"The coffee was fine. Nothing else, thank you, Mrs. Claybourne."

"Oh, but these are especially delicious. Perhaps you'd like to take some of them home for your family. Children do love sweets, don't they." She put down her cup. "I'll just have Dewey make up a package—"

John wasn't sure why, but anger suddenly rose inside of him. His wife was lying in bed and was likely to be crippled the rest of her life; he had a truckload of firewood that he couldn't sell; and two tires that were so bad he probably couldn't deliver the wood even if he could sell it. And Mrs. Claybourne, who had never missed a meal in her life, was offering him cream puffs to take home to his children. They probably cost ten cents apiece.

"Please don't, Mrs. Claybourne. I really don't want the cream puffs." He put his napkin back on the tray. "And I've got lots of things to do today, so I think I'd better get started."

He tried to keep the anger out of his voice. But for an instant she looked startled. Then her smile quickly returned. "How selfish of me. I sometimes forget how much providing for that big family of yours must take. I'm sure you must be the busiest man in the whole county, Mr. Walton."

"Well, not quite, Mrs. Claybourne."

She moved toward the door with him. "Will you be going past the post office on your way home, Mr. Walton?"

"You mean Ike's store? Yes, I reckon I will."

"I wonder if you would be good enough to mail some letters for us. Stuart Lee completely forgot them when he left this morning. I don't know what's gotten into that boy. But they say if you want something done, give the job to the busiest man around."

"I'll be glad to take them, Mrs. Claybourne."

"I would appreciate it. I'll give them to Dewey for you. And do give my best to Mrs. Walton."

After she glided away toward the front of the house, he went to the kitchen.

Dewey had the whole sink full of silver now, moving it from one side to the other as he polished it. As far as John could tell, both sides looked clean and sparkling.

"Got a big party comen up, Dewey?"

The old man laughed. "No, just doen my regular polishen, Mr. Walton. Rain or shine, party or no party, the silver gets polished every week. Ain't been no parties around this house since long before Mr. Claybourne passed over. But this ol' silver gets polished anyhow. I take it all down from the shelf, give it a good shine and put it all back again. Fact is, most of it hasn't been used in years.

John looked at the array of trays and goblets and candleholders, and then saw an equal supply in a walk-in closet next to the pantry. He smiled. "They ought to melt it down into silver dollars."

"If somebody did that, I don't reckon they'd even miss it, Mr. Walton. And it would sure save me a lot of work every week."

John laughed and got his tools out. Now that he knew exactly what had to be done, the job wouldn't take long. He pulled the refrigerator out and loosened the motor-mount bolts so he could get in behind it.

"You reckon Stuart Lee'll be comen home pretty soon, Dewey?"

"Oh, that's not likely, Mr. Walton. That boy, he goes racen all over the country with that Miss Weatherby. Lord, I'd just like to have the money he spends on gasoline."

"So would I, Dewey." While he worked, John thought about Mrs. Claybourne and the cream puffs Stuart Lee brought up from Richmond. It was strange how people spent money. And all that silver they never used. And the Packard roadster. But as the old saying went, "Easy come, easy go."

There were several versions of how the Claybournes originally got their money—none of them very flattering. Apparently most of it came from old General Harlan McKelvey, whose noble portrait stood over the fireplace. The most frequently told story was that after the Civil War he worked with carpetbaggers from the north, and through some questionable legal tactics, took over a number of cotton plantations in South Carolina and Georgia. From there the McKelvey empire expanded into banking and cotton speculation, and somewhere along the way became respectable. There were plenty of families like that in the South, John supposed. There were plenty of families like that all over the country. Sometimes it seemed like all the great fortunes in the world got started with some kind of larceny. When you thought about it, maybe it wasn't so surprising the country was in such bad shape.

Dewey was gone when John finished. The silver was all polished and standing neatly on the closet shelves, and a packet of letters was resting on the sink.

John got the refrigerator back in place. He tossed his tools back into his box and stood for a minute, wiping his hands, looking at the silver closet. There, sparkling in the soft light, the fifty or sixty pieces on those shelves represented about three years of cash income for the Walton family. And the Claybournes didn't even use it.

John smiled. If he owned something that valuable it would already be on his truck, and he would be headed for a pawn shop. He tossed the dirty rag into the toolbox and snapped it shut. Then he looked at the silver again, thinking about Stuart Lee's one-dollar payment for his work.

IV

John-Boy was amazed at the number of students there were milling around the college campus. Even more amazing was how carefree they looked. The girls all wore sweaters and pleated skirts and were remarkably pretty, and the boys had a rich casual air about them as they strolled to their classes or stretched out on the broad, tree-shaded lawns.

Sheriff Bridges had given him a ride down to the college. John-Boy had stopped by Ike Godsey's to see if there was any mail, and Ep was just leaving for Charlottesville. He would probably be there a couple hours, he said, and he would be glad to leave John-Boy at the college and pick him up later.

"Kind of early in the year to be goen off to college, ain't it, John-Boy?" Ep asked on the way down.

"I just want to find out what courses they got for next year. It was Mama's idea mostly. Now that she's sick I guess about the only thing she thinks about is getten us all started out on some kind of career."

"Well if your Mama's decided you're goen to go to college, John-Boy, I don't guess there'll be much doubt about it."

John-Boy wondered just how much truth there really was in that statement. There were probably a million young men graduating from high school this year whose mothers wanted them to go on to college. And very few of them would make it. But for the time being, going through the motions and getting a catalogue would probably make his mother happy.

'And right now that was about the most important thing.

Sheriff Bridges left him a block from the administration building, and John-Boy made his way along the walk feeling conspicuously out of place in his faded coveralls. In addition to the problem of money, he found it hard to imagine himself as one of these confident, pipe-smoking young men. He strode purposefully along, hoping he at least looked like he halfway belonged, and made his way up the steps and into the admissions office.

A broad counter stacked with brochures greeted him. Behind that, four young ladies, apparently students, were busily typing. John-Boy glanced over the literature and smiled at the closest girl.

"Could you maybe help me, please?"

"Certainly." She came quickly to her feet and looked him over. "You're new here, aren't you?"

"Well, I'm not really here. I mean I'm not really here yet. I just wanted to talk."

She leaned forward on the counter and smiled. "OK. What do you want to talk about? There's a dance next Saturday night. You got a date yet?"

John-Boy felt blood creep warmly up his neck. Maybe he wouldn't be so out of place here after all. She was an awfully pretty girl, with silky brown hair and greenish eyes. "Well, mostly I wanted to talk about how you register. And how much everythen costs and what courses there are and everythen."

The girl looked disappointed. But she quickly smiled and brought a catalogue from under the counter. "There you are. Everything's in that catalogue—fees, tuition costs, schedules of classes, and an entrance application. And help yourself to any of these brochures."

"Are they free?"

"Sure. Will you be starting in the spring?"

"Well, maybe. Or maybe in September. This is sort of long-range planning."

"Huh. Well, I'm not sure I can wait that long. What's your name?"

John-Boy blushed again. "John Walton, Jr."

"OK, John Walton, Jr., we'll look forward to seeing you. You think you'll be free for the Halloween dance?"

John-Boy had never experienced such forthright friendliness. Especially from pretty girls. "Well, yes, I reckon."

"OK, then it's a date. I'll see you in October."

"OK—uh, thanks for the brochures."

"You're welcome."

John-Boy hesitated at the door. The idea had been brooding in his mind for some time now—ever since that night Jason, Ben, and Jim-Bob came to his room. But he wasn't sure he had the nerve to do it. Or if it would even lead to anything.

"What's the matter?" the girl smiled.

"Well, I was just wondering. Do you have a medical school here?"

"A medical school. I would have guessed you were more of an Arts and Humanities type."

"You're right. I'm interested in a career in Journalism. But my mother's sick, and I wanted to see if I could get to talk to somebody."

"Your mother's sick? How?"

"The polio."

"Oh. Then you should see Dr. Miller in Experimental Medicine. Just go out the door, turn left and keep walking. You can't miss it."

"Thanks. Thanks a lot."

John-Boy followed the directions to a building that was newer than the one he had just left. In the lobby a listing of faculty members directed him to a small third-floor office where he found the door open. The man behind the desk looked huge, with muscular shoulders, disheveled hair and his necktie loosened and hanging crooked. He was only about thirty-five, John-Boy guessed, and he was scrawling notes across what looked like students' papers. John-Boy knocked lightly.

"Sir? Do you mind if I come in?"

The man didn't look up. "Door's open, you can come in. Door's shut, you can't."

John-Boy moved hesitantly to the desk. "My name is John Walton, sir. I'm not a student here."

The man continued marking papers. "Well, you're not alone, Walton. I've got a lot of people coming to my classes who aren't students either." He gave John-Boy a sharp glance. "Sit down, you're making me nervous."

John-Boy sat down. "I just wanted to ask you a couple questions, sir. The girl at the admissions office told me you might know something about polio."

"She did, huh."

"Yes, sir. And I wanted to find out if there are any new treatments, or any kind of medicine that can help somebody who's got it."

"Who's got it?"

"My mother."

The man stopped marking papers and gave him a long look. "What's your name again?"

"Walton, sir. John Walton."

"And you say you're not a student here?"

"No sir. I'm still in high school. But I'd like to come here some day—if we can get the money together. I thought you might talk to me anyway. You see—"

"Where you from?"

"Walton's Mountain. It's a little—"

The man grinned. He tossed his pen down and sat back. "Walton's Mountain!" He laughed. "You don't have to tell me where that is. My wife and I drive up there every fall to see the turning leaves. Mr. Walton, I want to thank you for giving us both a great deal of pleasure."

John-Boy relaxed a little. He'd never seen such a stern and gruff man undergo such an abrupt change. "Well, I don't reckon I can take credit for the turnen leaves. But the dogwoods and red-buds'll be bloomen soon. And the trees freshenen green. Springtime."

"I know. I come from Crabtree Falls."

John-Boy nodded. "Well, anyway, as I was sayen, my mother got polio about a week ago. She's over the fever now, but I think she's still got a lot of pain. I mean she tries to be cheerful and hide it from us, but sometimes—"

Dr. Miller was nodding. "She's in pain, all right. And it's going to hurt for a long time. Tell me the details. How long did the fever last, and how much can she move now?"

John-Boy told him everything he knew, including her efforts to sit up by herself. Dr. Miller listened thoughtfully, and then John-Boy had the shock of his life.

John-Boy hadn't noticed anything unusual when he came in. Just as Dr. Miller was a large man, so was his desk, and John-Boy had paid little attention to the chair behind it. But the doctor's hands suddenly dropped out of sight and then he swivelled and was propelling himself around the desk in a wheelchair. John-Boy knew his mouth must have dropped open a foot.

Dr. Miller frowned curiously at him, then laughed. "Oh, you didn't know?"

"No. I thought—I mean you were behind the desk."

"Don't be embarrassed, Walton. I'm not."

"But you looked so big. So strong."

"I am strong. At least half of me is."

In spite of the doctor's casual attitude toward his affliction, John-Boy was still flustered. He didn't know what to say.

"I've been scooten around in this little buggy for sixteen years now," Dr. Miller smiled. "It keeps me in shape. But I know exactly what your mother's going through. I was eighteen when it happened to me." He laughed. "The hottest halfback on any football field in Virginia. And probably the cockiest. Then, one Saturday, after another Miller triumph, I had these strange pains in my back. Sunday I was completely paralyzed from the waist down."

"That's how it was with my mother."

"That's the pattern. And we stand by helplessly and hope for the best. What's your mother's doctor done so far?"

"Well, he says there isn't any medicine. He put splints on her legs today."

"He's right about the medicine. And leg splints are the accepted approach. Nobody knows whether it really helps." He smiled ruefully and rubbed his chin.

"Dr. Miller, my teacher in Walton's Mountain, Miss Hunter, she says she read in the newspaper about a new treatment a woman has—someone called her Sister Kenny."

"Oh, yes, the Australian nurse. We're just starting to check into her methods. She claims an extraordinary recovery rate. But so far there's been no scientific verification of her claims. This doesn't mean her treatment doesn't work, of course. Only that she hasn't conducted them under scientific controls that would prove her claims one way or the other. She's attracted quite a bit of controversy."

"Is there any place I could find out more about her and the treatment?"

"Well, the fact is nobody knows a whole lot about it yet."

"Do you know where she is in Australia? Some place I could write to her?"

Dr. Miller thought for a minute, then suddenly swung the wheelchair and moved back behind his desk. "Tell you what—you leave me your name and address. I'll try to get hold of a couple pamphlets that detail her procedures and mail them to you. At least you can show them to your doctor and see what he thinks."

"I'll be enduren grateful to you, Doctor."

"No trouble. We're all in this together. I just wish I could get up there and examine her myself. You say she can sit up already?"

"Almost. She's worken hard at it."

"Mrs. Walton sounds like quite a lady."

"She is."

Dr. Miller smiled and stuck out a big calloused hand. "And I think you're quite a young man, Walton. I'm glad you came in. And I'm going to look forward to seeing you around the campus here."

John-Boy felt good when Sheriff Bridges picked him up. He knew he shouldn't let his hopes about the Sister Kenny treatment get too high. But at least he was doing something. The worst part of the last few days had been the feeling of helplessness—that there was nothing they could do but sit by and watch their mother suffer.

And he was also pleased with what he had seen of the Boatwright College campus. He didn't feel nearly so out of place when he came out of the medical building and crossed the campus again. Imagine that girl in the admissions office asking him if he had a date for the dance!

"What you smilen about, John-Boy?"

"Oh, I don't know. I just got a feelen things are goen to get better, Sheriff."

Ep nodded. "Well, maybe you're right. Can't see how they can get any worse."

John-Boy was a little disappointed not to see his father's truck when Sheriff Bridges dropped him off at home. Grandpa and Ben had the saw going, pushing a huge log through, and Jason was sitting on a woodpile plucking his guitar.

"Hey, John-Boy," Grandpa said, "you're just the man we're looken for. These logs are heavy."

John-Boy put his catalogue and brochures aside and stepped in beside Ben. "How about Jason? He don't look so busy."

When they finished the cut, Grandpa shut down the saw motor and sighted along the smooth edge. "Oh, we can't expect a great musician and guitar player to risk getten splinters in his fingers. No sir, Jason Walton's done all the hard labor he's ever gonna do in his life. So don't anybody go asken him to pick up a broom or carry in any stovewood."

They all grinned and Jason struck a loud chord on his guitar. "I'm gonna win that contest, Grandpa. Then I'll carry all the wood you want."

Grandpa snorted. "You win that contest and you'll be expecten breakfast in bed."

"Yeah, at ten o'clock in the mornen," Ben said. He smiled at John-Boy. "I got an answer from the magazine company today, John-Boy. They're senden me two dozen magazines, and they should be here tomorrow."

"Hey, that's great!"

"With nobody havin' any money, don't know who you're goen to sell 'em to," Grandpa muttered. "OK, let's run this log through again."

They slid the log back and made a second cut. "Where you been, John-Boy?" Grandpa asked when they finished.

John-Boy told them about his conversation with Dr. Miller, and that the man was going to send them pamphlets.

"You say this fella's crippled himself?"

"Yes, but he got the polio twenty years ago, Grandpa. Sister Kenny's only been doen her treatments a few years. And even Dr. Miller thought it was a good idea to find out what she does."

"You mean maybe Mama can be cured and walk again?" Ben asked.

"Well, now we shouldn't get too excited about this," Grandpa cautioned. "And it might not be a good idea to let your mother hear about it until Dr. Vance looks at them pamphlets. I reckon you'd better talk it over with your father first, John-Boy."

"How's Mama feelen?"

"She hates those splints," Jason said.

Ben nodded. "And she's gonna hate getten in a wheelchair even more."

"Well, those are things everybody's just goen to have to face," Grandpa said. "We can hope for some kind of miracle cure, and maybe it can even happen. But don't forget your Mama's havin' a lot of pain. Let's not encourage her to do a lot of exercises, or take treatments that are gonna make it worse for her." Grandpa suddenly had a gravely serious look. "And there's somethen else I think every one of us ought to reflect on. Nothen would break your mother's heart faster than havin' everyone expect her to come out of this all healthy and walken again—and then her not doen it. She'd figure she let us all down." He gave each of them a solemn look and then smiled. "Now, how about if we get this log cut up?"

Grandpa's statement jarred John-Boy a little. He knew there was a lot of truth in it and he felt a little ashamed that he hadn't thought things through that far. It would be terrible if she went through all kinds of tortures to please them, and then nothing happened. He resolved to be more cautious about his enthusiasms.

They had finished the timber and were cleaning up the scraps of bark when John finally got home. The truck came rattling around the dirt drive and squealed to a stop, and he swung easily down from the cab.

"Hey, Daddy, you got some new tires!"

It was the first thing John-Boy noticed. The last time he had driven the truck was when he fetched the doctor, and he had driven most of the way on a flat.

"Well, they're not exactly new," John said, "but for two dollars apiece they're not bad."

"You sell some wood, Daddy?" Jason asked.

The truck was still heaped with firewood.

"No. But I put that new part in the Claybournes' refrigerator this afternoon." He reached in and got a package from the cab.

John-Boy had no reason to question his father's answer. He had fixed the Claybournes' refrigerator, and they had paid him enough to buy new tires. It was more than a week later, when he was forced to think back to this moment, that he realized his father had not said exactly that. And everyone's attention was quickly distracted by the package.

"What is it, Daddy?" Ben asked.

"Oh, I just got your Mama a little present to lift her spirits a little. It's what they call a bedjacket. What you all cutten up out here?"

"We got two more of them timbers ready for Halverson, John."

"That's fine, Pa."

The bedjacket brought tears to Olivia's eyes. "It's just beautiful! It's the most beautiful thing I've ever seen! Where in the world did you ever get it?"

"I had it specially made in Paris, France," John grinned. "I told 'em what you looked like and asked 'em to make somethen just as pretty. That's why the color just matches your eyes."

The jacket was blue, made from a shiny quilted material, and had white, lacy trim. More tears streamed down her cheeks as she held it out and admired it. She finally put it on, and got a big kiss from John.

"Now," she said, "because you got me such a nice present, I'm goen to show you all how easy it is for me to sit up by myself."

"Now, take it easy, Livvy," John cautioned.

Erin had propped her up with pillows. Olivia tossed them aside and let herself drop flat to the bed. She smiled at them and began the struggle. She got an elbow beneath her. Then she swung herself halfway up, grimacing with the effort.

John-Boy held his breath, remembering Grandpa's words about encouraging her too much. The struggle was clearly painful.

She finally managed to get the arm straightened behind her. Then, after a deep breath and a single heave, she was up. "There!" she said triumphantly.

Everyone smiled with relief.

"Well, I declare!" Grandma exclaimed.

"That's marvelous, Mama," Mary Ellen said.

But it was apparent how much the effort had cost. Olivia's supporting arm began to quiver. John and Erin jumped forward and got the pillows behind her for support.

"Well," Olivia smiled, catching her breath, "at least I did it."

"That's real good, daughter," Grandpa said, "but you don't want to be overdoen it."

"I'm not overdoen it, Grandpa. And I've got to strengthen my muscles."

"Well nobody's expecten you to be walken by Easter."

Grandpa made the statement lightly, with no thought of how far off Easter was. Olivia suddenly brightened. "That's exactly what I'm aimen for, Grandpa. Easter."

"Well, now, Livvy—" John said.

"No, I've already decided. I want to walk to Easter sunrise services."

"That's only three weeks off," Grandma said.

"Three weeks and two days," Olivia smiled.

The announcement was a surprise to everyone. Until this minute they all assumed her ultimate objective was to learn to sit up without too much struggling. Dr. Vance had pointed out that this would be hard enough—and even dangerous. But walking, at least in his opinion, was out of the question.

"Do you have any feelen in your legs at all?" John asked.

"Not yet. But it'll come." She dismissed the subject with a smile. "Well, I've given my performance for the day. Now it's your turn. John-Boy, Erin told me you went to the college today. Did you get a catalogue?"

The question took John-Boy by surprise. "Well, yes. It's in my room."

"All right, we'll look at it tomorrow. Jason, have you been practicen?"

"Yes'm."

Mary Ellen suddenly smiled at John-Boy. "You're supposed to teach me to dance, John-Boy."

"What?! Me? I don't know anythen about dancen."

Olivia laughed. "All you have to do, John-Boy, is be her partner so she can practice."

"But, Mama—"

"And I don't see why we can't start right now. Jason, why don't you get your harmonica so we'll have some music."

It was clear that Mary Ellen wished she hadn't brought up the subject. "Right now, Mama? With everybody watchen?"

"Everybody'll be watchen when you go to the dance. You might as well get used to it right now."

Those not involved smiled, and Jason went for his harmonica.

"But, Mama," Mary Ellen protested again, "it's my turn to wash the dishes."

Grandma got up and headed for the door. "Don't worry about that, child, I'll do 'em. Don't know as I want to look at this anyway."

As far as John-Boy was concerned, the whole dancing lesson was a disaster. His sister, he decided, was constitutionally incapable of following anybody else's lead. Jason started with a waltz, and with John-Boy's first effort to glide Mary Ellen across the floor she pushed his arm away. "Quit haulen at me!"

From there it got worse. When John-Boy turned one way, Mary Ellen turned the other, bringing a thudding collision. And trying to move her with a graceful swing was more like a contest at arm wrestling. When Jason's laughter finally stopped the music Mary Ellen gave it up.

"It doesn't make sense, Mama. How am I supposed to know when he's gonna turn, or start backwards or frontwards, or somethen?"

For the moment, Olivia had no explanation. But it had been good entertainment. "I think you've done very well for your first lesson, darling. And you, too, John-Boy."

Earlier in the week, when Ben talked to his mother about becoming a magazine salesman, he had been bursting with confidence. He imagined himself going to every house in Walton's Mountain—maybe even going down to Charlottesville—and walking away from every door with his pockets full of dimes and quarters. Even Ike Godsey, who was an experienced businessman, had told him he would make a cracker-jack salesman. Last summer Ben had caught a whopping big fish and sold it to Ike for fifteen cents. And Ike didn't even like fish. So he should have no problems selling magazines.

But then, after he sent the letter to the magazine distributor, the doubts and uncertainty began. Did he really *sell* that fish to Ike? Or was Ike just being nice to him? Or was the fish worth more than fifteen cents, and Ike had turned around and made a big profit by reselling it? And magazines might be different from fish. Fish was food, and everybody needed food. But did anybody really need magazines?

Grandpa's statement had been the clincher, sending tremors of doubt and fear down Ben's spine. "With nobody havin' any money, don't know who you're goen to sell 'em to," he had said. People not having any money was something Ben hadn't even considered before. Why would they buy magazines when they couldn't even pay their light bills or buy food?

Ben had smiled through the clumsy efforts his brother and sister made at dancing, and then tried to shrug off his mother's question.

"I reckon they're sending me some magazines pretty soon. I don't know when they'll be here."

"You told me they were comen tomorrow," John-Boy said.

"Well, yes, that's what they said. But sometimes the mail is late."

"Oh, I'm sure they'll be here." Olivia smiled. "And I bet you'll be the best salesman they ever had."

Ben had nodded and tried to smile, but by the time he went to bed that night he found himself hoping the distributing company had forgotten about him, or that the mail arrived a week too late. Nobody could be expected to sell a week-old magazine. Or maybe they would come postage-due. Or maybe the magazine company would demand payment in advance—something he could not possibly do.

Other disastrous possibilities occurred to Ben as he trudged down to Ike's store the next morning. The man who brought the mail to Ike's might have car trouble and never get there. Or the freight train that brought the magazines from New York to Richmond could have gone off a bridge, or had a head-on collision with a northbound passenger train. As he moved up the steps of Ike's store, Ben had a clear picture of a shattered freight car lying at the bottom of a deep ravine. Bundles of magazines were scattered down the mountain slope, and tongues of flame were just beginning to lick at them.

"Hey, Ben, how you doen?"

Ike was behind the counter, transferring cans of soup from a carton to the shelf.

"Okay, Ike, how you doen?'

"Real good. How's your mama?"

"Feelen better. She's sitten up now."

"Hey, that's good news! And what can I do for you this mornen?"

Ben glanced at the caged area that served as the United States Post Office. As far as he could see, there were no packages on the counter.

"Oh, nothen, Ike. Just thought I'd come down in case there was any mail."

Ike put the last of the cans on the shelf and tossed the empty carton aside. "Well, let's just take a look. Mail came in just a few minutes ago. Haven't even looked at it myself." He lifted a big rope-tied bundle from under the cash register and put it on the counter.

Ben's heart sank. A large brown package made up most of the bundle. Ike cut the rope and smiled.

"Hey, look at that! To Benjamin Walton from the Seaboard Distributing Company. And it's heavy."

"Yeah. Well, it's just some old magazines I ordered."

"Oh, yeah?" Ike looked through the letters. "That's all there is."

"There's no postage due on this is there, Ike?"

"Nope. It's all yours, free and clear."

Ben gazed at the package without touching it. There was no question about it being the magazines. And they had suffered from neither train wreck nor fire.

"What's the matter, Ben? You don't have to take it if you don't want. I can mark it 'Return to Sender.' "

"No. I reckon I'll take it." Ben dragged the package off the counter and headed reluctantly for the door. "I'll see you later, Ike."

It was a warm, sunny day outside. But to Ben it seemed like the gloomiest day of his life. At the first large tree, he sat down, plopped the package between his legs and undid the knots of twine.

The magazines were all there; six copies each of *Liberty*, *Colliers*, *The Saturday Evening Post*, and *Literary Digest*. There was also a canvas bag with a shoulder strap, along with a letter and a packet of literature. Ben silently read it all.

"Congratulations," the letter began. "You have now taken your first step toward becoming an independent businessman. Enclosed are enough magazines to get you started—but remember, this is only the start! Set your goals high! Map out your territory and work it systematically! Don't be discouraged by potential customers who say no—go back week after week! You'll be amazed by the number of people who say *yes* on the second, third, or fourth call. Be industrious and persistent, and we guarantee your sales volume will rise and rise and rise week after week."

The brochures were full of testimonials from other magazine salesmen, all telling how easy it had been to make sales, and how pleased they were with their growing bank accounts: ". . . can't tell you how thrilled I am . . . expect to have enough profits to start college next year." E. W., STAPELTON, NEBRASKA. ". . . and when people heard I was the local salesman, they started calling me at home to order subscriptions!" A. H., TYLER, TEXAS. "I was discouraged at first, but repeat calls made all the difference. Thanks again for wonderful opportunity to become independent." C.G.D., ARLINGTON, GA.

Ben had some skepticism about those statements. They all might have been made long before the Depression. But the last brochure caught his attention, and he studied it closely. *The Art of Magazine Salesmanship*, it was entitled. "The magazines you now have in your hand" it began, "are beautifully bound collections of stories and articles and photographs, all printed on the best paper available. But this is not what you are going to sell! *No*, sir! You, Mr. Magazine Salesman, are selling *culture*! You are selling the most valuable collection in the world today—information, education, and wisdom!

"Ask your prospective customer if he is a community leader. Ask if he understands the government's fiscal policy, if he knows what kind of rifle should be used for polar bear hunting in Alaska, or if he knows what Babe Ruth eats for breakfast. When questions such as these come up at social gatherings, who do people turn to for the answers? They turn to the alert, informed, well-read members of the community—those who subscribe to your magazines! And that, Mr. Magazine Salesman, is what you are selling! You are not selling a magazine—you are selling its benefits! For the small cost of a year's subscription to these periodicals, you are giving your customers the respect, admiration, and approbation of their friends and neighbors."

Ben wasn't too sure he understood all that. He tried to imagine such ideas applied to his sale of the fish to Ike Godsey, but he had no success. Ike, he guessed, bought the fish because he was hungry—or because he thought he could make a profit selling it to someone else. He doubted if Ike's friends respected or admired him any more for having bought it.

Still, magazines were different. Maybe people did buy them for those reasons. Ben got to his feet. He shoved all the magazines into the canvas bag and slung it over his shoulder.

The Claybournes? If anyone in Walton's Mountain could afford to buy any magazines it would be them. On the other hand, the Baldwin sisters' house was closer. And Ben wasn't sure he could ask the Claybournes questions about polar bear rifles and Babe Ruth's breakfast.

He took a fortifying breath and headed for the Baldwins'.

V

"Why look who's here, sister," Miss Emily exclaimed, "It's young Benjamin Walton! Do come in, Benjamin. What a pleasure and delight to have you come a-callen."

Ben hated the name Benjamin. But he smiled and went in. "How are you, Miss Emily? And Miss Mamie?"

Miss Mamie was in the loveseat by the fire, a piece of needlepoint in her lap. "Oh, we're just fine, Benjamin. We were just talken about your dear mother and her tragic affliction."

"Now, you just sit down right here, Benjamin, and tell us all about it. We only just heard two days ago. I declare, I just can't tell you how distraught we've been."

Ben hadn't counted on the long questioning and the ladies' tearful demands that he tell them every little detail of his mother's condition. Then Miss Emily brought cookies and lemonade, and the two sisters told him about every illness that had ever been suffered by members of the Baldwin family. It was an impressive number.

"I declare," Miss Mamie finally concluded, "sometimes I just can't understand the intentions of the Lord at all. First, Papa died in the very prime of his life. He was only sixty-three, you know, Benjamin."

"Sixty-four," Miss Emily said with a smile.

"I do believe it was sixty-three, sister," Miss Mamie smiled in return. "But no matter. If you could have

71

seen him, Benjamin, you'd have sworn he was no more than fifty. Just as handsome and virile as any man you've ever seen. And the good Lord, just as mysterious as you can imagine, just struck him down in a most mystifyin manner. And now your poor dear mother!"

"Well," Ben shrugged. "I reckon we can be real grateful it wasn't worse."

Miss Emily sighed. "Now isn't that just like a Walton! Looken at the brighter side of things. I've always said, Mamie, if everyone in the world was as cheerful in the face of adversity as the Waltons are, the world would be ever so much more—more cheerful."

Ben smiled and nodded, not certain if this was exactly the right time to bring up the reason for his visit.

"Do have some more cookies, Benjamin."

"And lemonade."

"Well, I expect I've had about enough for right now." He shifted his bag to his lap. "And, as a matter of fact, the reason I came out here was to—to show you somethen."

"Oh, look at that, sister, Benjamin has a magazine."

"Are you sellen magazines, Benjamin?"

Ben glanced uncertainly at them. "Uh—well, as a matter of fact, no."

"Oh," they both said. They seemed disappointed.

"No, what I'm sellen, Miss Mamie and Miss Emily, is culture. Uh—information and education and wisdom."

"Oh, dear." They both looked puzzled.

"For example," Ben went on, "at a social gatheren, a party, when somebody asks a lot of questions, who answers them?"

They thought for a minute. "Well, it seems to me it's usually second cousin Homer Lee Baldwin. Wouldn't you say so, Emily?"

"Yes, Cousin Homer Lee does talk a great deal. But I'd say Cousin Oswald is more likely to answer questions. He has an entire record of the family tree, you know." She frowned. "What sort of questions did you have in mind, Benjamin?"

Ben had a feeling things weren't going exactly the way they were supposed to. "Well, questions about the government's fiscal policy. Or maybe what Babe Ruth ate for breakfast."

They stared silently at him.

"Or what kind of rifles they use in Alaska," Ben added weakly. "For shootin polar bears."

"Oh, dear! You mean those beautiful animals with the lovely white fur?"

"Yes."

"I think that's just terrible. Don't you, sister?"

Miss Mamie shook her head. "I declare, I can't imagine anybody doen such a thing."

Ben swallowed hard. He glanced at the magazine on his lap and those still in the bag. "Well—I reckon that isn't what I really came to talk to you about. What I wanted to say is that I've got some magazines here, and they're really very good magazines. In fact I was looken at some of them on the way out here, and they've got some real good stories in them."

"How exciten!" Miss Emily exclaimed.

"Yes. And actually, the reason I'm here is to offer you ladies a unique opportunity. You see, I represent these periodicals, which are the finest now bein' published in this country. In fact I'd say they are about the most highly regarded publications in the world."

"Think of that!" Miss Mamie said.

"And now," Ben continued, "for a limited time only, I can make an exceptional offer to a few very carefully chosen persons among the well-read people in our community."

They moved to the edge of their chairs. "And we're among the well-read persons you've chosen?"

It was coming easy now. Ben felt his voice change to a deeper, more authoritative tone. "Yes, ma'am. You and only a few others are bein' given the opportunity to have these stimulaten periodicals delivered to your door week after week for a full year."

"You'd be deliveren 'em personally?"

"That's correct. Now, this special offer is for all four magazines, and the cost is only five dollars. However, if you don't wish to purchase all four of them, we have another offer that—"

"We do," Miss Mamie said.

Ben stopped, his train of thought suddenly lost. "You do what, Miss Mamie?"

"We do want the special offer. We want all four magazines."

Ben's heart leaped in his chest. "You do?"

Miss Emily nodded agreement. "I was sayen to sister only last evenen—we're so out of touch with today's world. The dear Brontë sisters are wonderfully reassuren. But we should take time to acquaint ourselves with the here and now. And here, this mornen, you stand with the perfect solution!"

"You really want all four?"

"Oh, yes. What did you say the magazines were again?"

"Uh—*The Saturday Evening Post, Liberty, Colliers,* and *Literary Digest.*"

"Oh, don't those sound marvelous, Emily. Such impressive names. And I think I have five dollars right here in my purse."

Ben didn't quite believe it. According to the sales brochure he had done everything wrong. But Miss Mamie brought out the five dollar bill and placed it on the table.

Ben had to borrow a pencil to write up the order. When he finished, he left a current copy of each of the magazines, and the ladies escorted him to the door.

"We're ever so grateful for you and your company selecten us, Benjamin. And we promise to read every one of your magazines cover to cover."

"I'm sure you'll enjoy 'em."

Miss Mamie suddenly gave her sister a questioning look. "Emily? Do you think we should tell Benjamin about the gift?"

"Oh, yes, let's do. He was so nice to come all the way out here to let us buy his magazines."

"Now, you've got to promise not to tell anyone, Benjamin. Especially your dear mother."

"Okay," Ben murmured.

"Well, yesterday we sent off to Richmond for a present to give to your mother."

"It's just the most wonderful thing! I know she's just goen to be just as excited as she can be."

"Shall we tell him what it is, sister?"

"Oh, no!" Miss Mamie exclaimed, "Let's have it be a surprise for Benjamin too. A surprise for the whole family!"

"But we'll give you a little hint. You just try to picture what your dear mother would like more than anythen else in the entire world. The very thing that would make her the happiest right now."

Ben knew very well what would make his mother happier than anything—to be able to get out of bed and walk. But he didn't think there was anything in Richmond that would help her do that.

"Aren't you excited, Benjamin?"

"Yes'm."

"Now, don't you go and tell anybody. It'll just be our secret."

Ben nodded, uncertain what it was he wasn't supposed to tell anybody.

"And don't you forget to deliver our magazines next week."

"I won't."

Walking home, Ben tried to imagine what the Baldwin sisters' gift might be, but he gave it up. He finally smiled to himself, thinking about the sale he had made. Grandpa would be even more surprised than he had been. And his mother would be the happiest of all. He was a good salesman. In fact he could probably become the best magazine salesman in the whole country. Then the brochures would have new quotes: "I was discouraged at first. But through diligence and hard work I sold four full-year subscriptions on my first call. With my earnings I am now paying all my mother's doctor bills, and I will have enough left over for college." B. W., WALTON'S MOUNTAIN, VIRGINIA.

It was a busy morning at the Walton house. The first visitor was Miss Hunter, who brought a huge pot of stew for the family, and an orange cake and a whole box full of books for Olivia. As quickly as she left, Reverend Fordwick and Mrs. Brimmer arrived with the signature quilt the ladies of the church had been working on. Olivia was thrilled, and everyone in the family came up to look at the quilt.

All of this activity made it almost impossible for Elizabeth and Jim-Bob to get the kitchen floor scrubbed and polished, and for Grandma to get the washing done. It was lunchtime when Reverend Fordwick and Mrs. Brimmer left, and then Ben came bursting into the house with the startling news that he had sold four magazine subscriptions. Olivia had finished lunch and was scheduled for her nap, but no one had the heart to stop Ben from going up to tell her of his triumph. When he came back down he went directly for his canvas bag and headed for the door.

"Where you goen, young man?" Grandma demanded.

"I still got twenty magazines to sell. And I'm not hungry at all, Grandma."

John smiled and pointed to a chair. "Sit down, Ben. I know they're all goen to be very disappointed, but I think the people of Walton's Mountain can wait another ten minutes for your sales pitch."

The fourth visitor was a complete surprise to John-Boy. After his trip to Boatwright College and his talk with Dr. Miller, John-Boy's initial excitement had waned considerably. Thinking back on the conversation, he realized the doctor had promised to do nothing more than to try and get some pamphlets about the Sister Kenny treatment. And even if he

were successful, there was no guarantee that the treatment would help his mother—or even that the doctor
would approve of the treatments. At best, John-Boy
expected the pamphlets to come in the mail, along
with a letter expressing the doctor's opinion of them.
The last thing he expected was a visit from the doctor
himself.

But suddenly he appeared. A big black sedan rolled
quietly to a stop behind his father's truck, and a
blond-haired young man who looked like a football
player jumped out from behind the wheel and hurried
around to help the doctor out of the back seat.

John turned off the saw, and they all stared while
the young man set up some kind of collapsible wheelchair and half lifted the doctor into it.

"This the Waltons' house?" the doctor's voice
boomed.

John-Boy was speechless.

"Yes, it is," his father said. "I'm John Walton. Can
I help you?"

"Daddy," John-Boy stammered, "it's Dr. Miller.
The doctor I told you about at the college."

Dr. Miller grinned and rolled his wheelchair forward. "Huh! I thought this young fellow's name was
John Walton. Now which one of you is the real
one?"

John explained the difference, and Dr. Miller introduced Tom Hartman, his assistant. After the young
man shook hands, he retreated a couple steps as if he
knew the doctor wanted no one hovering over him.

"That address you gave me, John-Boy," the doctor
said, "got me only as far as a place called Ike Godsey's. But it was a treat to visit an old-fashioned country store again. What're you building out here, Mr.
Walton?"

John laughed. "Nothen, really. That's my business—cutten wood."

"You're a lucky man." The doctor smiled. "Say, I'd
sure enjoy a cup of coffee after my long trip."

"I would too," John grinned.

Tom Hartman lingered a few feet behind until the doctor had propelled himself to the back door. Then he stepped forward and swung the wheelchair up the steps in one motion.

Apparently, everyone in the house except Olivia was watching from the kitchen window. They were all standing just inside the door, and Grandpa rushed forward to help the doctor.

Dr. Miller waved him off. "I'm fine, I'm fine. Once I'm over the steps, the only thing you have to do is keep out of my way."

John introduced everyone and Grandma got the coffee pot going.

"You've got a fine looking family here, Mr. Walton. Having been an only child, I'm envious." He leaned to the side for a better view of Elizabeth. "And you're the youngest, eh, young lady?"

John-Boy hadn't realized it, but both Elizabeth and Jim-Bob had retreated almost to the living room, watching the doctor with a mixture of awe and concern. In their minds, this was the condition their mother would be in shortly. Elizabeth responded with a shy nod.

The doctor patted the side of his wheelchair. "You ever seen one of these things before?"

She shook her head.

"Well, they're a lot faster than they look. In fact, the other day I beat Tom here in a hundred-yard dash. And he's on the college track team."

Elizabeth and Jim-Bob smiled.

Grandma served the coffee, and Tom removed a chair so Dr. Miller could swing himself close to the table.

"Well, I guess John-Boy told you all about our conversation the other day, and the pamphlets I wanted to get for you." He brought some papers from his jacket pocket. "I got them quicker than I expected, but I know how important each day seems when you're first trying to work your way back. So I decided to deliver them in person."

"We sure appreciate it," John said.

"I appreciate having an excuse to come up to such beautiful country." His smile faded and he spread the pamphlets on the table, regarding them solemnly for a minute.

Grandma quietly took a chair, and the doctor now had everyone's breathless attention.

"What this woman has to say is very interesting. But I must tell you her treatment is also a very radical departure from the methods now being used."

"You said she doesn't believe in splints?" John-Boy asked.

"No, she doesn't. She insists that instead of preventing muscle damage, as most doctors believe, the splints can cause it. As I understand it, she thinks the muscles go into a sort of spasm and need to be relaxed with hot compresses."

Grandma nodded. "Now that makes sense to me."

Dr. Miller smiled. "It's not so different from the kind of treatment doctors might have prescribed a thousand years ago. But that doesn't mean it's bad. Modern practitioners can still learn a lot from folk medicine. Sister Kenny uses pieces of wool blanket wrung out in boiling water. Then, once the muscles relax, she starts massaging them. The idea is to keep the pathways from the brain to the muscles open."

Grandpa frowned. "But Dr. Vance said the nerves are dead and can't be regenerated."

"Yes, that's possible. But it's also possible the nerves could atrophy, or die, from lack of use. Unfortunately, we just don't know enough about what really happens."

"Well, the heat and massage sounds reasonable to me," Grandma said conclusively.

Dr. Miller nodded. "Many of my colleagues say it's far too simple. You understand, of course, that ultimately it's up to your family doctor. If he sees merit in it—" He shrugged.

"We'll get the pamphlets to him right away," John-Boy said.

John frowned and gazed across the table. "Doctor, what is your personal opinion? If Livvy was your patient, would you go ahead and try this Kenny treatment?"

The question brought a wry smile to the doctor's face. "You put me in a very awkward position, Mr. Walton. In a way, I'm in the same spot you are. There's nothing I'd rather see than the reports of a full-scale, scientific test of Sister Kenny's practices. I'd like to know for certain if they are one hundred percent successful, or sixty percent, or forty percent successful. Or if they are totally useless. Or even harmful. Unfortunately, there just hasn't been any scientific testing done at all. Thus no such reports exist. Therefore, my opinion has no more merit than does that of your wife's doctor. In fact, as applied to her, my opinion probably has even less merit. At least he has been attending her and knows exactly how the disease has progressed."

There wasn't anyone at the table who hadn't hoped he would say the Kenny treatment was good, or might be good, or that at least it was worth a try.

Dr. Miller saw their disappointment. "I'm sorry. I wish I could have brought you more encouraging news. I wish I could have brought you a bottle of medicine that would have her out of bed and walking in twenty-four hours. I think one of the most painful things a doctor has to do is caution patients against putting too much faith in experimental medicines or treatments. As scientists, we really have no choice. And as a doctor, I can make no judgment on something like the Sister Kenny treatment. All I can tell you are the facts as we know them right now. And that isn't much. Sister Kenny claims a high rate of recovery, but there is no proof to back up her claims. In time, no doubt, her claims will be investigated. Then we'll have enough information on which to make recommendations."

John nodded. "We appreciate you're bein' honest about it."

It was no more, nor any less than they should have expected. It was about the same thing Dr. Miller had told John-Boy at the college. But it was still disappointing.

Dr. Miller smiled. "Do you think Mrs. Walton might feel up to seeing me for a few minutes?"

"I think she'd enjoy talken to you, Doctor," John said.

Grandma looked at Erin, then nodded. "I reckon she's probably awake by now."

John-Boy gathered the pamphlets as the others rose. "Daddy? I could take the truck and get these over to Dr. Vance real quick."

"I think that's a good idea, son."

Dr. Miller's assistant helped him up the stairs. Then, only John and Erin accompanied him inside. Olivia was sitting up in bed, and showed no surprise at the entrance of a man in a wheelchair.

"John-Boy told me all about you." She smiled after John introduced them.

"He told me all about you, too."

Dr. Miller made no effort to examine her, but asked detailed questions about how she felt and how much she could move her limbs. Olivia demonstrated, making unsteady, almost imperceptible movements of her legs. Then, in the same circumspect terms he used downstairs, Dr. Miller discussed the Sister Kenny treatment. When he finished, Olivia smiled stoically.

"Then it's up to Dr. Vance?"

"Yes. You know, Mrs. Walton, the movement you can make with your legs is very encouraging."

Olivia laughed. "I'm glad you could even see it. I thought maybe it was just in my imagination."

"No, I could see it, all right. And I'm not speaking so much as a doctor right now. I'm remembering when I was in your place. I couldn't do that for months."

"I've been exercising. If I keep it up, I'll build up more and more control, don't you think?"

Olivia's enthusiasm seemed to alarm the doctor.

"It's certainly possible," he said tentatively. Then he gave her a sympathetic smile. "I know. You want more than 'possibilities.' You want certainties. I'm afraid there just aren't any with polio, Mrs. Walton."

Watching from across the bed, John felt a wave of compassion for Olivia. He wished the doctor would tell her something positive; encourage her with the exercises, or tell her there was even a slim chance of recovery. But he understood the doctor's cautiousness.

"It's natural for you to want to get back to the person you were before this happened," Dr. Miller said. "But you should be realistic and accept the fact that there are other possibilities."

"You mean I should be willen to settle for less than that?" Olivia asked.

"No, not for less. But maybe for something different." He suddenly smiled, as if reflecting on his own situation. "It's really not so bad, Mrs. Walton."

It was easy to forget that Dr. Miller was crippled and permanently confined to a wheelchair. His inner strength and commanding manner gave the impression of energetic virility. The subtle reminder of his real condition brought a faint blush to Olivia's cheeks.

"I'm sorry, doctor. And I do appreciate your comen to see me."

He waved aside the apology. "Mrs. Walton, I'm looking forward to the day you'll be coming to see me."

John waited until they were downstairs and out to the car before he asked the question. "Doctor Miller, do you think the movement in Livvy's legs means there's some hope?"

The man considered the question for some time. "It's possible, Mr. Walton. On the other hand, every case is different." He shook his head and smiled. "The only thing I can say for sure is that if determination and persistence are a factor in a person's recovery, your wife's got as good a chance as anybody I've ever seen."

John nodded, but the doctor looked troubled, as if he had more on his mind.

"Mr. Walton, I realize how much you and your family hoped the Sister Kenny treatment might turn out to be a miracle cure for Mrs. Walton. And I can see that from your viewpoint I sounded very negative about it. But I think you are a realistic man. You know that nothing is ever pure white or pure black. So I'll say this off the record—and with not a whole lot of scientific evidence to back it up. Personally, I don't see how the Sister Kenny treatment can do any harm. And with your wife's attitude, it just might be the right combination to bring off some kind of a miracle."

John was surprised by the statement. He also appreciated how difficult it was for the man to make it. "But you don't think I should tell Livvy."

"No, I don't. People react differently to doctors' advice. Some become so dependent on it they make no effort on their own. Others—sometimes because they have no faith in doctors at all—bring about their own cures through sheer determination. They just say to themselves they'll be damned if they'll let any bug interfere with their lives. Your wife is a strong woman. I think she just might be better off making the decision on her own rather than depending on someone else's opinion."

"What if Dr. Vance recommends against the treatment?"

"If he does, I would consider his advice very seriously. But in the end it's still her decision. And it's possible that Dr. Vance might think the treatment has a great deal to offer. It wouldn't surprise me if he endorsed it wholeheartedly."

John nodded. "Yes, I reckon that's possible." It would certainly simplify things, he reflected.

The doctor suddenly smiled. "Mr. Walton, you've got a fine family. I can't tell you how much I was impressed by that oldest boy of yours. And no matter how all this comes out, you've still got something very valuable in this house. Your wife's illness isn't going to change that."

The statement was both flattering and mildly pessimistic. Before John could respond to it, the doctor waved and the car pulled away.

VI

Dr. Miller's visit seemed to have settled nothing. If anything, John-Boy had the feeling the doctor thought his mother should try and make the best of spending her life in a wheelchair. And John-Boy got little encouragement when he delivered the pamphlets to Dr. Vance. The doctor had come out to his crowded waiting room for only a minute, and was puzzled by the literature.

"It's about the Sister Kenny treatment," John-Boy explained, "Dr. Miller at Boatwright College got the pamphlets for us, and he thought you might be interested in readin 'em."

"Oh, I see. You mean for your mother."

"Yes sir."

The doctor nodded and slid the pamphlets into the pocket of his smock. "Is she having any discomfort from the splints?"

"No, sir."

"That's good. I'll be over to see her tomorrow."

"We'd appreciate it if you'd read the pamphlets, Dr. Vance."

"I will." He gave John-Boy a distracted smile and disappeared.

The next morning John-Boy had another surprise.

As far back as he could remember, the only occasions on which his father ever went to church were Christmas and sometimes Easter—or when some friend or relative died. But after the dishes were washed and

dried and John-Boy headed up the stairs to get ready
for church, he met his father coming down the hall
wearing a suit and a necktie. He looked as casual
about his appearance as if he dressed that way every
day.

"You goen to church, Daddy?"

"Yep," his father said and went on down the stairs.

Only Erin stayed home with Olivia, and until all
the kids got in back of the truck and they drove off,
no one said a word.

"How come Daddy's goen to church?" Elizabeth finally asked.

"I reckon he just feels like it," John-Boy shrugged,
and the subject was dropped.

In the church nobody questioned his presence. It
seemed like his singing voice boomed out louder than
all the rest of the congregation put together, and his
"Amens" at the end of prayers were emphatic and
conclusive. When the service was over he politely answered questions about Olivia for five minutes, and
then they all marched to the truck and returned
home.

Until they had climbed out of the truck, none of
the children noticed Dr. Vance's car parked near the
porch. Then, knowing they would soon hear the crit-
ical decision, they went quickly inside.

Dr. Vance was waiting for them in the kitchen.
The pamphlets were on the table, and he smiled
through the greetings. Still, John-Boy felt a stab of
apprehension. Beneath the polite smile, Dr. Vance
didn't look too happy.

John pulled out a chair. "Sit down, Doc. Grandma,
you want to make some coffee?"

John-Boy and Grandpa also eased into chairs, while
the others stood near the sink. Dr. Vance fingered the
pamphets for a minute and then pushed them aside.

"Your daughter told me you'd be home shortly,"
he said, "So I haven't discussed these with Mrs. Walton yet."

"I take it you're not in favor of the Sister Kenny treatment, Dr. Vance."

It seemed to John-Boy that there was an odd note in his father's voice. It was not impatience so much as a quiet determination—as if he had made some important decision and he was intent on carrying it through.

The doctor sighed heavily and shook his head. "It's not only me, Mr. Walton. I talked to two other doctors last night after your son left the pamphlets. One of them is a physiotherapist and the other is an orthopedic surgeon in Richmond. Frankly, two of us were dead-set against it. The third felt that there was a possibility that the treatment might have some merit. However, even he felt that the risks might far outweigh the possible benefits."

"What's a physiotherapist?" Grandpa asked.

Dr. Vance smiled. "Oddly enough, it's a man who does exactly the kind of treatment this Sister Kenny prescribes. Principally, he works with people who have had badly broken bones, or people who may have had physical defects from birth. Through massage and a combination of heat and water treatments he attempts to strengthen muscles to correct the defects."

"Is he the one who thought the Kenny treatment might be good?" John asked.

"Yes. And he's also the one who warned against the risks. You see, physiotherapy can be a very complicated procedure, and requires considerable knowledge of muscular balance. In most cases, therapists are working with only one limb and a limited number of muscles. In the case of polio there is a massive atrophication. An attempt to properly strengthen all the muscles would necessarily be a very lengthy and complicated procedure. It would require a great deal of equipment, and expert supervision."

"Could it be done in a hospital in Richmond?"

Dr. Vance shook his head. "I asked Dr. Pierce the same question. He said he wouldn't attempt it. Aside from the complexity of the problem, it is still highly doubtful that the muscles would respond to the treatment. You see, there's still a fact we must face, Mr. Walton. The nerves are probably suffering from permanent damage. In the majority of polio patients that is the case. Under such circumstances no amount of massage or physiotherapy could ever revitalize them."

"And you think Livvy's nerves have been damaged that much?"

Dr. Vance nodded grimly. "I've tested and retested her reflexes right from the start. There's no doubt in my mind. In her case I'd say the odds are overwhelmingly against any kind of recovery. That's the principle reason I would advise against the Kenny treatment. In the long run, starting a treatment like that would do nothing more than postpone her adjustment."

"Adjustment to what?"

Dr. Vance took another deep breath, as if hating what he had to say. "To being crippled, Mr. Walton. Sooner or later, your wife's going to have to face the fact that she'll never walk again. The longer she puts it off the more difficult it's going to be for her. I'm sorry it's necessary to be blunt, Mr. Walton. But Mrs. Walton has been crippled by a terrible disease. She must learn to accept that."

Far more than the words, it was the grim expression of the doctor's face that caused John-Boy's heart to sink. Grandma had served coffee, but no one touched it. At the sink Elizabeth was staring at the doctor, almost in tears.

"It's hard," Dr. Vance went on, "but it's true. She's got to accept it. She's got to get on with the job of shaping a life for herself with her new limitations."

"You mean a wheelchair?" Grandpa asked.

"I'm afraid that's precisely what I mean. Every single person who ever had polio probably believed sincerely that he was going to recover, and made some effort to use his legs and strengthen the muscles. And everyone of them would have been better off if he immediately accepted the fact that he was crippled and made the best of it. Believe me, Mr. Walton, your wife is no different. In the end, her efforts and her exercises will only prolong the adjustment."

John-Boy glanced at his father. He seemed to have stiffened in the face of the harsh words. He nodded toward the pamphlets.

"This Sister Kenny treatment—what are the risks involved?"

"In the first place," Dr. Vance said firmly, "the splints would have to be taken off in order to begin the treatment. This is extremely dangerous. Unsupported, the muscles are likely to pull the legs into gross deformity. Secondly, the treatments would be very painful. The motor nerves, which control leg movements, may be damaged, or totally destroyed. But the sensory nerves, which relay pain, can still be healthy enough to make the treatments unbearable." He shook his head. "But probably the worst part of all is giving her false hope. Believe me, Mr. Walton, if you looked around enough you could probably find a hundred different people claiming to have a cure for polio. There are thousands of quacks in the world who make fortunes by promising cures for incurable diseases. And unfortunately, there are thousands of patients spending millions of dollars going from one of these quacks to another."

"Doesn't appear to me this Sister Kenny woman's asken for any money," Grandpa said.

"No, I'll grant that. But it's still a false hope. People can have other reasons for promoting quack cures."

John gazed at the doctor for a long time. "Doc, would you come up and tell Livvy everythen you've told us? All about the risks, and about other people with polio thinken the same way she does?"

The doctor hesitated. "Yes. I did intend to examine her today. But I think the decision is yours as much as hers, Mr. Walton. In her condition it's hard for your wife to be objective."

John nodded and rose. "I been thinken about it."

"I hate that man," Elizabeth said as quickly as John and the doctor were gone.

Grandma poured herself coffee and sat down. "Now, that's no way to talk. Particularly on the Sabbath."

"He's just doen what he thinks is right," Grandpa added.

"Do you think Mama will want to do it?" Mary Ellen asked.

Grandma shook her head. "I don't know, sweetheart. But that steam and massage—sounds to me like it's just what Livvy needs."

John-Boy didn't know what to think. If someone had asked him an hour ago, he would have been one hundred percent in favor of the treatment. But Dr. Vance's saying that everyone else who ever had polio was just as determined as his mother—that was a discouraging thought. And if the treatment didn't work, she would be crippled even worse.

John-Boy guessed the same thoughts were on everybody's mind as they waited. They all gazed silently at the table until Grandma finally got up.

"Well, I reckon I'd better fix us all some lunch."

Mary Ellen rose. "I'll help, Grandma."

After twenty minutes the doctor and John came down. But they went out the front door, and another five minutes passed before the sound of the doctor's car could be heard and John finally came in. He looked preoccupied. And still wearing his church clothes, he seemed more solemn than ever.

"Did he tell her, Daddy?" Jason asked.

He nodded and sat down to drink his cold coffee. "Yep, he told her everythen."

"What'd Mama say?"

John shook his head and gazed thoughtfully at the table. "She didn't say nothen. She's thinken about it."

"What do you think, Daddy?" Mary Ellen asked.

He considered the question for some time.

Grandma put her knife on the sink and came over to hear his answer.

"In the end," he said, "it's your mama's decision. I told her what I thought. And the doctor told her what she can expect if the treatment doesn't work. He also told her how painful the whole thing will be." He glanced at Grandpa. "Up till now I don't think Livvy understood all the risks a thing like this has."

"I think it would work," Grandma said. But her voice was not as confident as before.

John shook his head. "I reckon none of us can say anythen for sure. If Livvy wants to go ahead with it, we'll give her all the help we can. But if she decides against it, none of us better say anythen against her decision. Like Doc Vance says, we'll start right off helpen her make the adjustment." He looked around the table at each of them. "And nobody'll ever even think about what it might have been like if she had decided different."

They all nodded.

"I think you're right, John," Grandpa said. He glanced significantly at Grandma.

"Whatever Livvy says goes with me," she said emphatically. "Lord knows all the pain and sufferen she's already had. I ain't goen to add to it."

"Daddy?"

Erin was standing near the end of the table. Apparently she had come into the room without anybody seeing her.

"What is it, sweetheart?"

"Mama wants to see you. She wants all of us to come up."

John-Boy felt his heart drop. Apparently she had come to some decision. But John-Boy had given up any hope of guessing what it might be. And there was no clue in Erin's solemn expression.

They all rose. "Whatever she says," John cautioned again, "it's the right decision."

John-Boy lagged to the rear and found Ben at his side.

"I wish that doctor from the college had just said to go ahead with it," Ben whispered. "If he knew about the treatment when he first got sick, I'll bet he'd have done it."

John-Boy nodded. "I reckon we'd better not forget what Daddy said."

Ben shrugged and dropped the matter.

She was wearing her blue bedjacket when they came in. From her propped-up pillows she smiled at each of them, watching as they found places to sit.

"How was church?" she finally asked.

"Real nice," Grandma smiled, "and Reverend Fordwick delivered a real nice sermon. Don't you think so, John?"

"Well, now, Mama, I don't really have a lot to compare it to. But he sounded right sincere to me."

"What'd he talk about?"

"He talked about maken a lot of noise," Grandpa laughed. "And that husband of yours did just that."

Olivia smiled. "Psalms, ninety-seven! I love that. 'Make a joyful noise unto the Lord, all ye lands. Serve the Lord with gladness: come before his presence with singing'."

"Daddy sang louder than anybody," Elizabeth said.

John laughed and Olivia gazed at him with what seemed like more love than John-Boy had ever seen in anybody's eyes. "I'm glad," she said simply.

Suddenly John-Boy had a feeling that everything was going to be all right. No matter what his mother decided, everybody was going to do his best to make it work.

"Well," she said lightly and smoothed the new signature quilt over her lap. "I had a very nice talk with Dr. Vance. He said that if we tried somethen like the Sister Kenny treatment these splints would have to come off my legs. And if that was done there would be a chance of my legs getten—getten worse. But I reckon he told you all this already. He also said the treatments might hurt a little bit. In fact, I guess he doesn't want me to try the treatments, because he said it would hurt a whole lot."

She paused, but nobody made a sound.

"I reckon the only thing that's worryen me is that—I mean if I went ahead with the treatment—is that it might be a whole lot of trouble for all of you."

"Don't you even think about that, little girl," Grandpa said quickly.

She gave an embarrassed laugh and looked around at all of them. "Then I'd like to do it."

John-Boy wasn't aware of the fact that he had quit breathing. A wave of relief suddenly flooded through him; his father and everyone else in the room were grinning, and Elizabeth made a dash into her mother's arms.

"Mama, I know you're gonna get better," Elizabeth blurted out, "and we're goen to help you. We're goen to help you every day, and do all those things to make you get better no matter what we have to do."

"That's right, Mama," Jason added, and Ben and the other children nodded agreement, none of them trusting their voices.

"Don't see how anyone could help but see the good sense in putten hot foments on a person's ailen muscles." Grandma grinned. "We shoulda been doen it right from the start."

John-Boy guessed his father was the happiest of all of them. There seemed to be big portions of pride and love and determination all mixed into his smile as he gazed at Olivia. He was silent while the others expressed approval of the decision. Then he leaned forward in his chair.

"Well, Livvy, when would you like to get started?"

She shrugged and looked down at her legs. "Seein' as how it's everybody else who'll be doen the work, it's up to you."

"Right now!" Jim-Bob said.

"Yes," the others chroused.

"Let's take the splints off, Mama?"

"There's an old wool blanket in the linen closet," Mary Ellen said. "Shall we start cutten it up?"

"Now, hold on a minute," Grandpa said, "We can start doen all them things quick enough. But I reckon your Daddy'll want to read over them pamphlets first and make sure we'll be doen things just right. And I guess your Mama doesn't want all of us staren at her while she gets them splints taken off. So how about if your Daddy and Grandma stay here and take care of that while the rest of us go down and get things started."

John smiled. "Sounds like a good idea, Pa."

Elizabeth gave her father a questioning look. "Daddy? What will Dr. Vance say if we take the splints off?"

"Well, sweetheart, I wouldn't worry about it. Fact is, I kind of think he had an idea what was goen to happen when he left here today."

"What'd he say, Daddy?" John-Boy asked.

"Nothen exactly straight out. But at his car he sort of said somethen about how medicine wasn't a real exact science, and sometimes doctors don't know why some people got cured. But he said he still didn't believe in miracles."

Grandma shook her head. "The poor man. That's exactly what happens when a person gets all that book-learnen."

Olivia grinned and they all laughed.

None of them expected any instant improvement in Olivia's condition. The pamphlets warned against it, suggesting it could be weeks before any signs of recovery became evident. The first step, which they continued for three days, involved only the wrapping of the legs in hot, wet strips of woolen blanket.

John-Boy's task was to keep a steady supply of stovewood coming. During the day his father cut logs into foot-long chunks, and when John-Boy got home from school he split these into stove kindling and stacked them close to the back door. Ben and Jim-Bob transferred them to the kitchen, and were responsible for keeping the stove burning for a constant supply of hot water. Grandpa and Mary Ellen dipped the pieces of wool into the large cauldron of boiling water and put them through the wringer of the washing machine. With the damp strips still steaming, Jason and John-Boy quickly carried them upstairs in a wooden tub. There, Grandma, Erin and sometimes John, carefully wrapped the strips around Olivia's legs, at the same time removing the ones that had cooled. Elizabeth, who had the tenderest skin, tested the strips before they were applied, making certain they were not too hot.

The treatments did seem to be painful, but Olivia insisted that she could stand it. Rather than a burning sensation, she said there was a deep aching that ran all the way up her spine. But there was no change in the total numbness of her legs.

While the children were in school, John, Grandpa and Grandma managed to give her two treatments, and then two more lengthier treatments were given in the afternoon and evening.

In spite of all the activity, Olivia insisted that Jason continue practicing his guitar for the big amateur contest. And Ben managed to sell most of his magazines by calling on two or three people each day after school.

Surprisingly, it was G. W. Haines who provided Mary Ellen with time to work on her dress. His first reaction to her announcement that she was going to the dance with him was less than enthusiastic.

"What dance?"

"The school dance that's comen in two weeks. You asked me to go twice already."

"Oh, that dance. But I didn't think you'd really want to go."

"Then why'd you ask me?"

"Well, I just thought—I mean I thought you'd just like it if I asked you. You never wanted to go to any dances before."

"Well, I want to go to this one."

"But I've never been to a dance before."

"Neither have I."

G. W. scratched his head and put his hands in and out of his pockets, but couldn't think of any more arguments. Mary Ellen smiled, everything settled.

"So I gotta make this dress, and you gotta help me."

"I ain't doen no sewin on any dress."

"You don't have to. You just come over here a couple days a week and take my place wringen out these hot pieces of wool. That'll give me time to work on the dress."

G. W. was not certain about what he had committed himself to, but on those days he helped with the treatments he was an enthusiastic worker.

On Wednesday, the day they were scheduled to begin the massage and manipulation of the legs, John-Boy chopped the kindling hurriedly. When he finished, he stacked the pieces by the door, returned the ax to the barn, and then froze as he started back to the house.

"Well, I'm glad to find someone home. I've been knocking on the front door for five minutes."

It was Dr. Vance—smiling, standing by the back porch with his bag.

John-Boy knew his father was upstairs helping with the hot compresses. And the kitchen was in a state of chaos, with the last batch of wool strips being prepared.

"I reckon nobody heard you, Dr. Vance."

"I guess not." He smiled, waiting for John-Boy to escort him in. "How's your mother feeling?"

John-Boy didn't know what to say. There wasn't any noticeable improvement in her legs, but her spirits had risen considerably since the splints were taken off. "About the same, I reckon."

"Well, do you think she'd like to see me?"

"Uh—yes. Sure. Come on in."

John-Boy escorted him quickly through the kitchen. Grandpa and Jason looked up from their work and gaped for a second, but the doctor only had time to smile and nod at them.

"I'm not sure if she's awake or not," John-Boy said as they reached the top of the stairs. Then his heart dropped.

Lying on the floor a few feet from his mother's bedroom door were the old splints the doctor had so carefully put on her legs. Until last night they had been on the floor of the bedroom. Then his mother had asked that they be taken out, saying they depressed her every time she looked at them.

John-Boy tried to keep himself between the doctor and the splints as he stopped at the door.

"I'll just knock. I think Daddy might be in there."

"Fine."

"Daddy," John-Boy said as the door opened, "Dr. Vance is here."

His father stiffened. But he quickly smiled when he saw the doctor. "Come in, Doc. How are you?"

His father seemed to take the whole thing in stride, and his mother was smiling calmly from her bed.

"We've started the Kenny treatment, Doc, but so far we've only been doen the hot compresses. We figured we'd start the massagen this afternoon."

John-Boy couldn't help admiring his father's airy manner. From the way he made the announcement, it might have been a procedure prescribed by Dr. Vance himself. The doctor's cheerful smile faded a little. But if he had any feelings of anger he successfully hid them.

"I see. And how are you feeling, Mrs. Walton?" He glanced at the wooden tub and the disarray of damp woolen strips.

"I think I might have a little feelen in my legs, Dr. Vance. At least I seem to have a feelen that they're there now."

"That sounds encouraging."

"I can't wait to get started with the massagen."

Dr. Vance nodded and eased himself slowly into a chair. "I suppose there's no point in my telling you again about all the risks you're taking. I honestly don't think this is going to work, Mrs. Walton. And I think you should get those splints back on as quickly as possible." He sighed heavily. "However, I talked to Dr. Pierce again. I thought—I mean, on the chance you might go ahead with this, I asked him how he might proceed with such a treatment. Purely on a hypothetical basis, of course. He suggested that he would use a great deal of what they call a 'sleeve massage.' That is, in addition to a general massaging of the muscles, you work down the legs as if you were forcing all the blood to the toe. Then you work back up to the thigh in the same manner."

They all stared at him. John finally smiled. "We'll do that, Doc."

"You understand, of course, that I don't approve of this at all." He shook his head and rose, still holding his bag. "As long as you're feeling all right, I guess there's no point in my examining you, Mrs. Walton. I would advise, however, that you don't overdo these treatments so much you don't get enough rest. The body is still its own best healer. For that you need rest and sleep."

"We'll be careful," John said.

The doctor appeared ill at ease, as if not sure what else to say. He finally turned for the door. "Well, I'll be back to see you. And if you have any complications be sure and call."

"Dr. Vance?" Olivia said.

He paused at the door.

"Thank you very much."

A grin suddenly came to his face, but he waved and turned quickly away. "You're all busy—I'll see myself out."

There were a number of visitors during the week. But most of them came while John-Boy and the rest of the children were in school. The only evidence of their calls were delicious casseroles and desserts, along with fresh cut flowers or small gifts in their mother's room.

But the Baldwin sisters came late in the afternoon. John-Boy, Ben, and Jason were stacking wood when they heard the big Franklin car come grinding around the side of the house. It was going far too fast, and they all gasped as it swerved, narrowly missing the truck, and then came to a sliding stop with Miss Emily smiling happily from behind the wheel.

"Hello, John-Boy, Jason. And Benjamin! Oh, we're happy to see you're here."

Miss Mamie got out from the other side. "You didn't tell anybody about our secret, did you, Benjamin?"

Ben had completely forgotten about the Baldwin sisters' secret gift for his mother. "No, m'am, I didn't tell a soul."

Miss Mamie was out of the car too. "I told you he wouldn't tell, sister. And Ben, we just can't say how much we've enjoyed all our magazines."

"Read every word, and just loved them."

Ben nodded. "I reckon the next issues'll be here tomorrow."

"Oh, I just can't wait! But right now we've got just the most excitin news. Our surprise for your mother. came just today, and we've just come from picken it up at Mr. Godsey's store!"

"I know she's just goen to love it," Miss Emily bubbled. "And you big strong boys can help us carry it in. We've got it right here in the trunk of the car."

John-Boy smiled and they all moved to the back of the car. He couldn't imagine what could be so big it would require all three of them to carry it in. When they opened the trunk and he saw it, John-Boy paled. Beside him, both Ben and Jason stopped short and stared.

It was a wheelchair.

"Isn't it lovely?" Miss Emily exclaimed. "It's the very finest they had in the whole catalogue."

"We got the catalogue from the Richmond Surgical Supply Company," Miss Emily added. "Dr. Vance assured us it is a most reliable establishment."

John-Boy didn't know what to say. His brothers looked as sick as he felt.

"Dr. Vance?" he murmured.

"Oh, yes. We talked to him the minute we heard about your poor mother's affliction."

The statement relieved John-Boy a little. At least Dr. Vance had recommended it before his last visit. But he wondered about his mother's reaction. "Ben, maybe you—uh, ought to go get Grandpa to help us."

"Grandpa?"

John-Boy gave him a pleading look. "Yeah. I think he's in the kitchen." It was not Grandpa he wanted, but someone to warn everybody in the house about what was coming.

Ben blinked at him and finally understood. "Oh, yeah, Grandpa. Yeah, I'll get him."

The Baldwin sisters went on about all the special features of the wheelchair, and John-Boy took his time untying the cord that was securing it in the car's trunk.

"It sure looks nice," he said. "Jason, you want to get that side of it?"

It was a collapsible model, much like the one Dr. Miller had used. Jason still seemed to be in a state of shock, but they got the thing out. They had it open when Grandpa finally came.

Apparently Ben had passed on the news. Grandpa displayed no surprise, grinning all the way from the door.

"Well, well, well, what a pleasant surprise, havin' two lovely ladies come a-visiten. And look at that! Isn't that somethen! Why, I don't think I ever saw such a beautiful wheelchair in all my life!"

"Isn't it, though," Miss Emily agreed. "Why it just makes you want to sit down in it and never take another step for the rest of your life!"

"Emily!" Miss Mamie gasped, "that's just a terrible

thing to say. Don't you dare say such a thing to poor Mrs. Walton."

Miss Emily looked hurt. "I just meant—I'm terribly sorry if—did I say the wrong thing, Mr. Walton?"

"Of course you did!" Miss Mamie exclaimed.

Grandpa brushed it aside. "All with the best of intentions, Miss Emily. Don't give it another thought."

Miss Emily gave her sister a haughty look and smiled at Grandpa. "Thank you, Mr. Walton."

"Now, let's get this on into the kitchen, ladies. I sent Ben upstairs to see if Livvy's awake."

"I do hope she's not sleepen," Miss Emily sighed, "I'm just dyen to see the look on her face when she sees it."

"I'm pretty sure she's sleepen," Jason mumbled.

Because of their "recipe" making activities, and their infrequent appearances in church, Grandma had never been too fond of the Baldwin sisters. It was her belief that their not having husbands was a deprivation clearly arranged by the Lord himself. But she managed a smile when they came in the kitchen.

"How nice to see you, ladies. And isn't that a nice gift for Olivia."

Her icy tone was lost on the ladies. "Oh, we're so happy you like it, Mrs. Walton," Miss Mamie gushed.

"We think Mrs. Walton'll just be thrilled," Miss Emily added.

"I'm sure."

Ben arrived with a wooden smile. "Mama's awake and said she would like to see you ladies very much."

"You didn't tell her about our surprise, did you, Benajmin?"

Ben glanced at Grandpa who was holding a steady smile. "Uh—no. She's real anxious to see you. She's real glad you came."

"Isn't that sweet, Emily? I declare we really should come a-callen more often. And you should call on us some time, Mrs. Walton."

Grandma nodded, her tolerance fading.

"Well, I reckon we can go on up," Grandpa said and pushed the wheelchair forward.

"I do wish we had gotten a big ribbon for it," Miss Emily sighed.

John-Boy couldn't help admiring the self control his mother displayed. After her determined resolve to get back on her feet, and all the painful effort she had committed herself to, the presentation of a wheelchair must have been a bitter experience. It was like a prizefighter being presented with the loser's trophy just before the fight began. It made John-Boy wish the treatments of the last week had shown some evidence of progress.

John-Boy's father greeted the ladies warmly. Standing by the head of the bed, Erin smiled, and Olivia even managed to show some surprise when the chrome and leather chair was wheeled in.

"I just don't know how you're goen to get down the stairs," Miss Mamie said after they were seated. "But I'm sure these strong Walton men can carry you down to the wheelchair."

"Yes," Olivia smiled.

"And sister, isn't it just wonderful how Mrs. Walton is accepten her misfortune? Why, I declare, most people would just be feelen so sorry for themselves! But here she is just maken the best of everythen, just as happy and cheerful as can be."

"I was just readen yesterday in one of those magazines your Benjamin was so kind to let us purchase, that handicapped people in Des Moines, Iowa, do the most wonderful handicraft work. Was it Des Moines, Mamie?"

"I believe it was Davenport, sister."

"Well, no matter. They make baskets and the most lovely little potholders. And just imagine all the knitten you can do, Mrs. Walton. Why, I declare, the whole Walton family can have the nicest new sweaters and stockens!"

John-Boy looked anxiously at his mother. The smile was still fixed on her face, but her eyes seemed to

have dulled. He didn't guess she could take a whole
lot more of this.

" 'God's ways seem dark,' " Miss Mamie quoted
with a sigh, " 'but soon or late, They touch the shinen
hills of day.' "

"That's beautiful," Olivia said.

"Mr. John Greenleaf Whittier. One of our most
neglected poets. He's one of our favorites."

They all nodded. John finally cleared his throat.
"Ladies, it was real nice of you to come a-callen. I
reckon it's about time for Livvy's rest now."

They quickly rose. "Yes, and we must be goen."

"It was such a pleasure seein' you, Mrs. Walton.
And we do hope you'll be feelen up to usen your new
wheelchair soon."

Olivia mustered a final smile. "Thank you very
much for the gift. It was very thoughtful of you.
You're the best possible friends and neighbors."

Grandpa saw them out.

Until they heard the door close and the Baldwins'
car finally start up, everyone in the bedroom sat in
glum, reflective silence. Then John-Boy watched his
mother as she gazed at the glistening wheelchair. It
was the fate Dr. Vance had predicted for her, and the
one she was no doubt wondering about right now.

"They meant well, Livvy," John finally said.

She nodded. "They're really very sweet old ladies."
She struggled to sit up straighter in the bed. "It's all
right," she said and gave a short laugh. "But I do wish
somebody would get that silly thing out of here."
Her smile suddenly became an amused grin. "Put it
with the splints."

VII

The Biloxi Theater didn't look like much. The bricks were crumbling, and half the lightbulbs around the big marquee had been shattered a long time ago. Even the letters, which had been recently put in place, were a variety of sizes. They said: GIANT AMATEUR CONTEST.

John-Boy and Jason had looked at them for a while and then moved closer to read the printed poster mounted in the glass-covered case.

GIANT AMATEUR CONTEST
Saturday, March 24

Starring Radio's Greatest Talent Discoverer

OSGOOD TENNYSON

Exceptional Prizes!
First Prize:
Professional Guitar
Second Prize:
Complete Set of Fine China
Third Prize:
Miniature Golf Set

AUDITIONS NOW BEING HELD

Jason looked apprehensively past the empty box office to the darkened glass doors inside. "I don't know, John-Boy."

"You'll do fine. What're you worried about?"

"I'm not worried. It's just that—I mean it doesn't even look like anybody's here."

"They're probably around back, through the stage door."

Jason's nervousness had begun the minute they climbed into the truck and headed for Charlottesville. It had been a struggle getting him to go at all.

At first their father had intended going only as far as Ike's to do the shopping. Grandma needed some stew-beef, and Mary Ellen wanted ribbon for the finishing touches of her dress. Then Jim-Bob and Elizabeth asked to go along so they could get something for their mother, and John decided to go on to Charlottesville. He knew a place were they could buy a perfect present for Olivia.

Then John-Boy had joined them, and with a great deal of prodding they convinced Jason that he should bring his guitar along and try out for the amateur contest.

Jason thought it was too soon—that they probably weren't even having tryouts yet. And he really hadn't worked out the song he was going to play.

"John-Boy," he said now, "you know, playen for the family is one thing. But playen for somebody like Osgood Tennyson—well, you know he's used to hearen the best."

"You're one of the best. Come on."

"There's probably a hundred guitar players already tryen out. They're probably twice as good as I am."

"Don't you want to go in and find out?"

"Well, sure I do. Sort of. But I sort of don't, too."

John-Boy knew exactly how he felt. Standing up in front of a professional entertainer who broadcast a radio show to millions of people every week was likely to make anyone nervous. But he also knew Jason was very good. John-Boy shrugged. "Well, I reckon we can just wait out here for Daddy to pick us up again. Probably be a good idea not to mention all this to Mama, though."

John-Boy moved out to the curb and looked up the street as if searching for their father. He knew it was a little unfair mentioning their mother. But it was for her that Jason had started practicing the guitar in the first place.

"John-Boy?"

"Un-huh."

"Listen. As long as we're here—I reckon we might as well go on in."

"You sure you want to?"

"Yeah—well, yes. Yes, I want to do it, John-Boy."

John-Boy expected the stage to be all lit up, with dozens of hopeful contestants waiting to audition. But the place was deathly silent—as dark and cold as a tomb. Once their eyes adjusted, they made their way to the empty stage.

"Guess nobody's here," Jason said and turned back.

"Wait a minute. Let's try the other side."

When they reached the far side of the stage, Jason suddenly disappeared in the darkness. His guitar clattered to the floor.

"You all right?"

"I reckon." Jason picked himself up and retrieved the instrument. "Guess I tripped over some ropes."

"Hey! What're you kids doing back here?"

The voice was gruff and came from somewhere in the dim light ahead. They moved cautiously forward. An office door was open and a stocky little man was standing in front of it.

"Mr. Tennyson?"

"No. Whadya want?"

The man had garters on his shirtsleeves and the stump of an unlighted cigar was clamped in the corner of his mouth.

"We were looken for the place to audition for the amateur show."

The man looked them over and gestured irritably toward the office. "OK. In here."

The office looked worse than the rest of the building. Faded posters were tacked crookedly on the walls. Newspapers were scattered around, and a paper plate full of half eaten spareribs rested on a desk. Everything except the ribs was thick with dust.

"Where's Mr. Tennyson?" Jason asked.

The man sat down and took a bite from a rib. "He ain't here. Won't hit town till the day of the show."

"Oh."

"I'm Snyder, his advance man. What's your specialty?"

"Specialty?"

"Yeah." The man waved the rib impatiently. "You juggle—tap-dance—imitate Laurel and Hardy? What's your gimmick?"

John-Boy stepped aside so the man could see Jason's instrument. "My brother plays the guitar."

"Sensational," the man grunted, and concentrated on his sparerib.

"His name is Jason Walton."

The man pulled a copy of a newspaper closer so he could read it. "OK. Let's hear it."

Jason looked at John-Boy and back at the man. "Right now? In here?"

"You're gonna audition—so audition."

Jason looked around and found a place where he could lean on a chair and prop his foot up.

The man suddenly looked up. "Hold it. First let's have the entry fee."

"Entry fee?"

The man took another bite of rib and gazed at them through lidded eyes. "That's right."

"The poster didn't say anythen about an entrance fee," John-Boy protested.

"One buck—in advance. Everybody pays an entrance fee."

Jason looked at John-Boy, then shrugged. "Well, then, I reckon I can't audition. I don't have a dollar."

The man wiped his chin with a dirty handkerchief and looked at John-Boy. "How about you?"

"No, I don't either."

"Too bad, kid. That's show business." He took another bite and went back to his newspaper reading.

John-Boy was a little suspicious about the whole thing. But there wasn't much they could do. Jason moved past him to the door.

"Hold it," the man suddenly said. "Listen, kid, for you I'll make it fifty cents. Everybody's got fifty cents."

"We don't."

The man seemed to be more disappointed than they were. John-Boy turned. "C'mon, Jason. We'll just wait and audition for Mr. Tennyson."

"Program'll be all set when he gets to town," the man said quickly.

John-Boy smiled. "Then maybe the manager of this theater—or the newspaper. Maybe they'd like to listen to us."

It was an ambiguous threat that the man could take any way he chose. He understood it clearly enough. He gazed narrowly at John-Boy for a minute. "Aw, what the hell. Go ahead and play."

The song Jason had been practicing was one he had written himself after watching Grandma do her ironing. He called it "The Ironing Board Blues." Jason played and the man sat back and gazed at him as if wishing he was in New York City, or Miami—any place in the world except Charlottesville, Virginia. John-Boy had a feeling there would be the same reaction if Jason were playing a comb and tissue paper, or a fancy thousand-dollar violin. When Jason finished, the man picked up another rib and squinted at his newspaper.

"You're great, kid. Be here half an hour before show time."

Sheriff Ep Bridges didn't work any set hours. There wasn't a whole lot of crime in Walton's Mountain. But when anything did happen it was usually at night or during the early morning hours. So Ep had no guilt feelings about spending time at Ike Godsey's pool ta-

ble during the day. If no one called by nine in the
morning, he generally figured nothing had happened
during the night, and he wouldn't have any call to do
much until darkness came again. This was particularly
true on weekends. If anyone got drunk or disorderly,
it would most likely be on a Friday or Saturday
night, and those were his busiest times. Therefore, in
spite of the fact that he had no fixed days off, Ep tend-
ed to look on the daylight hours of the weekends as
periods of rest.

Thus he had a little feeling of resentment when, on
a Saturday morning, he found himself in his patrol car
heading out toward Claybourne Hall. Beside him was
Dewey Hamilton, who seemed so agitated he wasn't
making a whole lot of sense about what the complaint
was.

"You said there's some silver missing, Dewey. Now
just how much silver are you talken about? Is it just a
couple pieces, or a whole lot?"

"Far as I know, Sheriff, it's just them two pieces.
Least that's all Miz Claybourne talked about this morn-
en."

"When did she first miss it?"

"I don't know."

"Well, when did you first hear about it?"

"I first heard this mornen. Miz Claybourne asked
me to polish up them two goblets and put 'em out on
the sideboard, and I went to get 'em out of the cupboard and they wasn't there."

"Did you look anyplace else for 'em?"

"Oh, yes sir. We looked in every cupboard and
shelf in the whole kitchen and the dinen room and everywhere."

"Does Mrs. Claybourne have any idea who might
have taken them?"

This question seemed to disturb Dewey more than
anything else. He looked scared to death and he
shook his head. "I don't know, sir. I don't know
nothen about that. Miz Claybourne, she just told me

to come down and get the sheriff and I come. That's all I know."

Ep Bridges had his doubts about the silver pieces being lost. He had been in the Claybourne house only two or three times in his life, but he had seen enough silver, crystal, and knickknacks and china to know they probably didn't have the slightest idea how much of it there was. And two silver goblets could have gotten thrown out in the trash without anybody noticing.

Dewey had been almost apologetic in his request for Ep to come out to the Claybournes'. "If you don't mind, Mr. Sheriff, Miz Claybourne'd like you to come talk to her. She says if you can come real soon, she'd appreciate it."

It had taken five minutes of questioning before Dewey revealed that the silver was missing and that Mrs. Claybourne suspected that it might have been stolen.

Ep Bridges smiled wryly to himself as they drove the rest of the way in silence. If anyone were going to burglarize a house in Walton's Mountain, the Claybournes' would certainly be the place to pick. But it wouldn't make much sense for a burglar to take only a couple of silver goblets.

Ep parked his patrol car at the top of the curving driveway, just behind young Stuart Lee's Packard roadster. He was glad to see that Stuart Lee was home. The boy wasn't half the man his father had been, but he still might be easier to deal with than Mrs. Claybourne.

The family was gathered in the drawing room, sitting on the two sofas in front of the fireplace. Dewey escorted Ep through the door and then discreetly disappeared.

Mrs. Claybourne smiled, but it was tense. "I'm so glad you could come, Sheriff Bridges. You know my son and daughter, of course."

"Sure. How are you?"

"This is terribly embarrassing, Sheriff. And most awkward, I'm afraid."

"Now, mother—" Stuart Lee said.

"I'm sorry, dear, but we must face facts. And I think we can just let Sheriff Bridges draw his own conclusions."

"Thank you, ma'am. Dewey told me there are a couple of silver goblets missing."

Amelia Claybourne looked like she was bored with the whole thing and would rather be someplace else. Stuart Lee fidgeted impatiently.

"That's correct, Sheriff," Mrs. Claybourne said, "And they're not ordinary silver goblets by any means. They are Paul Revere silver that my grandmother owned and passed on to my mother. They're two of the finest pieces we own, Sheriff, and the only matching pair in the world is in the Boston Museum of Fine Arts."

"When did you first miss 'em?"

"Dewey searched all the cupboards this morning, and they simply aren't here, Sheriff. And there's no question in my mind but that they've been stolen. I saw them here only two weeks ago, and Dewey remembers polishing them just last week."

"Mother," Stuart Lee said, "it's quite possible they've been misplaced."

"But we've searched everywhere."

"Maybe they're in the attic," Amelia suggested.

"Darling, nobody has been in the attic for months. Now how in the world could they get up there?"

"Mrs. Claybourne, is there any evidence to indicate the house was broken into? Or have any strangers been here? Salesmen, or someone you don't know very well?"

"Nobody has broken in, Sheriff. But there has been someone here."

"Mother, I don't think—"

"Who do you mean, Mrs. Claybourne?"

"I'm not accusing anyone. Please understand that. But in the past week and a half the only person who's been in this house, aside from ourselves and Dewey, is John Walton."

For a minute Ep wasn't sure he had heard right. Or if he had, Mrs. Claybourne was certainly joking.

"John Walton?" Sheriff Bridges laughed. "Now, you're not really suggesten John Walton would take anythin, are you, Miz Claybourne?"

"I'm simply stating the facts, Sheriff. John Walton was here last week fixing the refrigerator. It just happens that Dewey was polishing the silver and had it all set out on the kitchen sink at the same time. And now two silver goblets are missing."

Ep sat back and rubbed his forehead. "Mrs. Claybourne, John Walton may have been in your house, and Dewey may have had all the silver out on the sink at the same time. But I ain't even goen to talk about the possibility of him havin' stolen those goblets."

"I agree, Sheriff, it's a terrible thought. But are you aware that Olivia Walton is terribly sick?"

Ep checked the anger that suddenly rose inside him. "I'm aware of it."

"The poor man—I'm sure he needs money desperately. And if he had asked, I would have gladly helped him with his doctor bills, or whatever he needs. But surely you can appreciate the temptation that valuable silver must have been for him."

"No, Mrs. Claybourne, I can't."

"Mama," Stuart Lee said, "just because John Walton was here does not mean we have conclusive evidence that he took the goblets."

Ep Bridges was glad Stuart Lee spoke up. He wasn't sure what would have come out of his own mouth if he had continued talking.

"I didn't say it was conclusive evidence. As distasteful as it is, I simply say there is no other explanation for their disappearance."

"Mrs. Claybourne," Ep said, "I think there are probably ten other possible explanations—including the possibility that they got thrown out in the trash by mistake."

"Are you saying Dewey is responsible?"

"No, I ain't sayen that. I'm just sayen somebody might have made a mistake."

Amelia laughed and made a statement that surprised Ep. "I think it's all very simple. I think Mr. Walton took the goblets on an impulse. I think he probably took them, and then regretted it ten minutes later. But then he couldn't very easily return them. So he probably took them to a pawn shop somewhere."

Mrs. Claybourne nodded. "I think that's a very plausible explanation, Sheriff."

Ep didn't know whether to tell them all to go to hell, or try to reason with them. But maybe people in their position never met or got to know men like John Walton.

Mrs. Claybourne smiled stiffly. "Sheriff, as I said, I can understand Mr. Walton's distress, and I sympathize with him deeply. I think it's quite possible that in this terrible ordeal of his wife's illness he simply isn't himself, and is not really responsible for his actions. I know how devastating polio can be. Mr. Claybourne's second cousin in Savannah had it. I know the terrible effect it had on the family. In light of that, Sheriff Bridges, it is not my wish that Mr. Walton be sent to jail, nor that he even be subjected to the humiliation of arrest. I simply want the goblets returned. Now, if you will inform him of that, and explain the consequences of his failure to return them, I am sure we can get all this settled with a minimum of fuss."

Ep took a deep breath and let it out slowly. The high and mighty Mrs. Carter Claybourne was so dead certain John Walton stole the goblets she was dictating the terms for their recovery. To his credit, Stuart Lee seemed to be embarrassed about what was going on.

Ep pulled himself slowly to his feet. "Mrs. Claybourne, I want you to think this over very carefully. Accusen a man of theft without knowen for sure he stole somethen is a very serious offense called defamation of character. So I'd caution you to be pretty sure about what you're sayen before you go on sayen it. And while you're thinken about everythen, I'd advise you to search this house from stem to stern. Then I'd also do some searchen in the trash and around the yard. . . ."

Mrs. Claybourne didn't look like she was accustomed to taking advice from small town sheriffs. "I have reported the loss of the goblets, Sheriff Bridges, and I have informed you of all the facts in the situation. Thus I think I have fulfilled my obligations. I will go further and remind you that I have been more than generous in outlining the conditions for the return of the goblets. All that remains, it seems to me, is for you to do your duty as a public servant and pursue your investigation in a direction that appears quite obvious." She gave him an icy smile and turned to her son. "Stuart Lee, will you please see Sheriff Bridges to the door?"

Ep didn't bother saying good-bye. Mrs. Claybourne lifted her chin and turned away, and didn't seem to expect it. He followed Stuart Lee to the front door.

"I'm sorry, Sheriff. I'm afraid my mother is more overwrought than the situation warrants."

"I'll agree with you there, Stuart Lee. But I'm tellen you right now, John Walton didn't take those goblets."

The boy forced a smile and nodded. But his heart didn't seem to be in it. Ep left him at the door and went down the steps to his car.

Was it possible, he wondered as he drove off and headed back toward Ike's? Was it even remotely conceivable that John Walton might have taken those goblets? As Amelia said, could he have done it in a moment of desperation and despair, and then regretted it five minutes later?

No, Ep told himself. If John Walton wasn't an honest man, then the good Lord hadn't gotten around to making any yet. No. Before John Walton ever stole from anyone, he'd walk into the poorhouse with empty pockets. And he'd do it with his head high.

Ep shook his head. He hoped to God he was right about that. The frightening part of the whole thing was that after being a law officer for so many years, Ep knew there was no way for certain of predicting human behavior. Under enough stress just about any human being could do things that would shock the Lord himself. And Ep really had no choice. As ridiculous as the accusation was, he had to check it out.

VIII

"You sure these'll bloom by Easter, Daddy?"

"Well, the man said if the weather stays warm there's a good chance."

"But they're so small!"

Crocuses were Olivia's favorite flowers, and they were John's recommendation as the perfect present for her. With the twenty cents Elizabeth and Jim-Bob brought along, and the eighty cents their father contributed, they brought more than a hundred sprouting bulbs home from Charlottesville. On the way home they had agreed that the best place to plant them was in front of the porch where Olivia could see them from her bedroom window. Grandpa was surpervising the planting, while Grandma, John, and John-Boy watched from the porch.

"Crocuses are always small," Grandma pointed out. "But so many of 'em, they're goen to be awful pretty."

"If they bloom," Jim-Bob said doubtfully.

"They'll bloom all right," Grandpa said. "Now get the hose, Elizabeth, and we'll give 'em a good soaken."

"You're not supposed to give 'em a good soaken," Grandma said, "They're only supposed to be damp."

"They gotta have water to grow, old woman."

"That soil's got plenty of water in it already. You soak 'em any more and the roots ain't got nothen to grab ahold of."

"I didn't say to flood 'em. I said soak 'em. That means just a light sprinklen."

116

John-Boy never got to hear the end of the dispute. His father nudged him and laughed. "C'mon, John-Boy. I reckon we'd better get a fire goen for your mother's treatment."

Olivia's treatments had now become a smooth, methodical operation. This afternoon, the compresses and then the massaging was all done with musical accompaniment. Jason's success at getting into the amateur contest had delighted Olivia. She made him tell the whole story twice, and then had him play her "Ironing Board Blues" over and over while the others worked on her legs.

At least once each day Grandma had been putting Olivia through a series of tests, watching carefully to see just how much movement she could accomplish in her legs. It seemed to John-Boy that the improvement—if there was any at all—was scarcely noticeable. The only change, it seemed, was that her efforts were getting progressively more painful.

"Daddy?" he asked later when they were working in the sawmill, "Do you think the treatments are really helpen Mama any?"

"It's hard to say, John-Boy. It's only been a week now."

From the tone of his answer it seemed clear that his father was also disheartened.

"Do you think because it's hurten more that maybe there's some improvement?"

"Yes, that may be. I hope so."

"And these things sometimes happen in spurts," Grandpa added. "It's like them crocuses we planted out there. Now, I reckon they're just goen to sit there awhile and do nothen, cause they get kind of a shock from bein' transplanted. The same thing's probably happenen with your mother. It'll take her legs a while to get adjusted to the treatments."

John gave him a sly smile. "Maybe we should be putten more water on Livvy's legs, Pa."

John-Boy laughed. "How much water did you end up putten on the crocuses, Grandpa?"

"Well, we soaked 'em real good. I'd say about one drop of water for each of 'em."

Laughing about the crocuses distracted them from the subject of Olivia's progress, but John-Boy knew that his father and grandfather were as concerned as he was. After they had run another log through the saw, Grandpa squinted toward the front of the house and smiled.

"Well, look who's here."

Ben was striding up the road, his canvas bag dangling from his arm. From his manner he looked like a determined young businessman on his way to an important meeting.

"Hey, Ben! Ain't you talken to us?"

Ben detoured from his path and came over. "I gotta write a letter real fast," he grinned. "I sold almost all my magazines and I gotta get some more."

"Did you deliver the Baldwin sisters' copies?"

"Sure. First thing. And I sold four more subscriptions to Ike Godsey."

"Well, I declare," Grandpa laughed, "I didn't even know Ike could read."

Ben gazed thoughtfully at him for a minute. "Grandpa, do you know who the secretary of state is?"

"The secretary of state? The secretary of what state?"

"Do you know who are the three most promisen young American writers?"

"Ben, I don't know what you're talken about. What are these young writers promisen to do?"

Ben dug some pamphlets out of his bag. "This week only, Grandpa, I've got a special offer that only a few people in this community are goen to have an opportunity to take advantage of. Now it just happens that you, Mr. Zebulon Walton, are one of those special few that have been selected. You are one of the leaders in this community who we feel will appreciate and benefit most from the subscriben to all four of these wonderful publications. Now, what I'm goen to do—"

John and John-Boy were laughing, and Grandpa shook his head. "Ben, you just better get on into the house and write that letter."

Ben grinned and headed for the door.

"Someday," Grandpa said, "that boy's goen to be the richest man in the world. I just hope I'll still be around to help him spend all that money."

If John-Boy knew of any way in the world he could set back the clock—or even eradicate a half hour entirely from his life—he guessed he would have chosen to do it late that afternoon when Sheriff Bridges showed up at the house. There had been times before when his father's behavior puzzled him—either for his lack of concern over what seemed like serious matters to John-Boy, or when his father was gravely worried about what appeared to be trivial questions. But the problem presented by Sheriff Bridges, and the manner in which his father handled it, left John-Boy completely dazed.

They were cutting the last log of the day, trimming and squaring it into a timber for Mr. Halverson, when the sheriff's patrol car rolled to a stop next to their old truck. There was nothing unusual about his coming out for a visit. Among his father's friends, John-Boy guessed Ep Bridges was one of the closest. But as quickly as he got out of his car, John-Boy had an ominous feeling. The sheriff moved slowly and his smile had a tightness that John-Boy had never seen before.

His father didn't seem to pay much attention. "Hey, Ep? How's it goen?" he called.

"Fair, John. How you doen, Zeb? John-Boy?"

"Oh, we're getten along," Grandpa smiled, "What brings you out here at this time of day?"

John laughed, cleaning the last of the sawdust off the table. "I reckon he figures it's suppertime, Pa. Ep don't get a whole lot of good home cooken, you know."

Ep smiled politely and glanced off at the house. "How's Livvy getten along?"

"Livvy's doen real good," Grandpa answered, "Says she's goen to walk by Easter time."

"That's good. I'm real glad to hear that."

"Then how come you're so down at the mouth?" John smiled. "You look like your best tracken dog just died, Ep."

John-Boy hadn't said a word. He knew from the start that something was on Sheriff Bridges' mind. Now the sheriff looked more uncomfortable than ever.

"John, there's somethen I'd like to talk to you about. Somethen I think maybe we'd best talk about in private."

John-Boy moved quickly. He was behind the saw table and he started around the side. Grandpa also turned to go.

"Now, wait a minute," John said. He laughed. "John-Boy's sixteen years old, Ep. And Pa's almost twice that. I don't reckon you can say anythen that'll embarrass 'em."

"John, it concerns you, and it concerns the law. I'm not sure you'd want 'em to hear it."

John-Boy saw his father stiffen. He guessed Sheriff Bridges couldn't have said anything stronger to guarantee their staying.

"I'm not sure what you're talken about, Ep. But I reckon now they'd better stay."

Sheriff Bridges knew he'd made a mistake. But it was too late to change it now.

"OK, John. I've got a simple question. I'd just like to know where you went after you left the Claybournes' a week ago Friday."

John-Boy saw the look of surprise on his father's face, and he tried to remember the day himself. His father had gone to fix the Claybournes' refrigerator. It was also the day John-Boy had gone to the college and talked to Dr. Miller. He could remember nothing special aside from that. But his father's surprise had suddenly turned to wary anger.

"That's a strange question, Ep. And that was more than a week ago."

"That's right. You head toward Charlottesville that day? Or maybe down to Richmond?"

"Ep, what's this all about?"

"John, I'm not maken any accusations. In fact, I think it's probably all some kind of misunderstanden. But I've just come from the Claybournes' house. They've got a couple of silver goblets missen."

John-Boy could hardly believe he had heard right. But the sheriff's meaning was clear. "Sheriff," he blurted out, "if you're sayen that—"

"Ep," his father interrupted, "why are you asken me about this?"

"I gotta ask, John. Accorden to Mrs. Claybourne, you're the only caller that's been to the house since they last saw those goblets. So she sent for me this mornen."

John-Boy knew his father was furious. But he was holding it in, trying to control himself. "Ep, I don't like what you seem to be getten at."

"Now, John—" Grandpa said.

"I wanta hear this, Pa! What're you sayen, Ep?"

"Now, take it easy, John. I don't like this any more than you do. And there's only one thing you gotta tell me. Where did you go that day after you left the Claybournes'?"

John-Boy wondered if his father even remembered where he had gone. But if that was the case, his father was too mad to say so.

"It's none of your business, Ep."

"All right, maybe it isn't. But I have to tell the Claybournes somethen. You tell me what to tell 'em."

"Tell 'em I don't have to talk to anybody about my private business."

John-Boy almost felt sorry for Ep Bridges. As much as he knew his father was innocent of anything, it would have been simple for him to say so and prove it. Sheriff Bridges shook his head.

"I don't think that'll satisfy 'em, John."

Grandpa was suddenly mad, too. "What do you mean by that?"

"Ep means I'm coveren up somethen," John said, "Lyen."

"Now, John—I'm just tellen you that Mrs. Claybourne has decided you must have taken the goblets. She figures you're short of cash because—because of doctor bills and all—and maybe you took them goblets out of desperation and hocked 'em."

John-Boy felt himself churning inside. That Mrs. Claybourne would even think of such a thing was infuriating. He couldn't imagine his father stealing anything under any circumstances.

"Ep," his father said more calmly, "that isn't what happened. This is crazy. You know that."

"Yes, I think I know that. But all I'm asken is for you to clear yourself."

"I don't have to tell you anythen, and I'm not goen to, Ep."

John-Boy couldn't restrain himself. "You know my daddy didn't take those goblets, Sheriff. And that's all that matters."

Ep sighed wearily. "John-Boy, I've known your daddy longer than you have, and almost as long as your Grandpa. But I wouldn't have believed any man could say he was a thief without John letten him have it."

John-Boy wasn't sure what that meant. Did the sheriff think that because his father hadn't hit him he was hiding something?

"Ep," John said coldly, "you'd better leave now."

Sheriff Bridges gazed silently back at him for a minute. He shook his head. "I don't like this, John. But you gotta appreciate the spot I'm in. Won't you please say somethen to protect yourself?"

"No."

"Daddy—"

"Get in the house, John-Boy. I don't want any more talk about this, Sheriff. And I think it's time we said goodnight."

"John—"

"I got nothen more to say."

Sheriff Bridges shook his head and turned away. "Goodnight, John. I'm around if you need me."

"Goodnight."

John-Boy had moved from the sawmill halfway to the house. He watched now as the sheriff got into his car and drove off.

"John—" Grandpa said, but he got no farther.

"I don't want to talk about it, Pa. And John-Boy, I told you to get in the house!"

John-Boy didn't know if it was hurt or anger that stabbed deepest at him as he went into the house. But he knew he was confused. He was almost trembling as he went through the kitchen and up to his room.

For almost an hour he stood numbly at the window staring out at the darkness. He found himself going over and over the entire conversation just to convince himself it had really taken place.

His father certainly hadn't taken those silver goblets. But why hadn't he said so? Why didn't he just tell Ep Bridges where he had gone that day after he left the Claybournes'?

But what confused and frightened him, and had left him totally speechless, was his father's sudden anger and the way it had turned on himself and Grandpa. In all the years. John-Boy could not remember him ever doing a thing like that.

After he had moved to his bed and lay down, a soft knock came on his door. It was Grandpa. He smiled as he came in and sat down, but he looked equally confused.

"You all right, John-Boy?"

"I reckon, Grandpa. But what's goen on? I've never seen Daddy act like that."

Grandpa shook his head. "I reckon he's had a lot to

worry about lately. This thing—whatever it is—just hit him at the wrong time."

John-Boy nodded, but it didn't seem like a very satisfactory answer.

"Your daddy's a proud man, John-Boy. But it's the kind of pride that sure wouldn't let him steal anythen from the Claybournes."

"I know that, Grandpa. But how come he didn't just tell Sheriff Bridges where he went that day?"

Grandpa shook his head, as baffled as John-Boy. "I reckon maybe it was partly Ep's fault. Bein' a sheriff he gets used to putten questions to people kind of harsh. He got your daddy's back up right from the start."

"But it sounded like Ep thought maybe there was a chance Daddy did take those goblets."

Grandpa nodded. "That's what I mean. Ep knows better. He shoulda made it clear he knows better right off. But it'll work out, John-Boy. You know, your daddy doesn't let on to you kids much—or even to Olivia. But he's got plenty of problems these days. After you go off to school, he's been out every day tryen to sell firewood, or hustle up money any way he can. And I mean honest money, John-Boy. But that ain't easy these days. And I guess there ain't nothen that can make a man feel like he ain't a man at all any more than not bein' able to feed his family.

"But Ep and your Daddy'll be getten together again. They'll be laughin over this whole thing soon enough."

From the anger he'd seen in his father's face, John-Boy wasn't too sure about that.

"What I wanted to say, John-Boy, is we shouldn't mention this to your mother or the rest of the kids. Livvy's feelen good now, and worken real hard at getten better. We don't want nothen like this disturben her."

"No," John-Boy agreed.

Grandpa rose and gave him a pat on the shoulder.

"And don't you worry about it too much. Things like this always work themselves out in time."

"I hope so, Grandpa."

"Supper'll be ready in a couple of minutes."

Neither John-Boy nor his father looked at each other at the table. But from his short answers, and the determined way he ate, John-Boy knew his father was still upset. After the dishes were cleared, his father said he would take care of chopping the kindling tonight. Then he disappeared through the back door.

John-Boy found his anger shifting heavily to the Claybournes—or at least to Mrs. Claybourne. Not only was it vicious and unfair of her to accuse his father of stealing, it was even worse to do it when his mother was sick with polio. How could anyone be so stupid and heartless at the same time? He found himself considering the possibility of marching over to her house and telling her exactly what he thought of her.

"John-Boy, what's the matter with you?" his mother asked when he was helping her with her exercises.

"Nothen, Mama."

She laughed. "You look like you just heard the world's comen to an end.

"I reckon I'm just tired, Mama."

"Well, you go on to bed. Grandma and I can do this. And Jason, if you'd get your guitar, I'd surely like to hear the "Ironing Board Blues" again. I think the rhythm helps my exercisen."

John-Boy was not surprised when his father didn't go to church the next day. After breakfast he went directly to the sawmill, and he was working hard when they all drove off. But John-Boy was surprised when they arrived at church. As far as he knew, none of the Claybournes had ever attended any of their church services. But in the front row, apparently all by herself, was Amelia.

Until a week ago, Amelia Claybourne had been going to a private school down in Richmond. But last Monday when John-Boy and his brothers and sisters arrived at school, Stuart Lee's roadster was parked outside, and Stuart Lee and his sister were talking to Miss Hunter, enrolling Amelia in the class.

Now, when he saw Amelia in church, John-Boy felt another wave of resentment toward the family. He and Mary Ellen had made a special effort to help Amelia in school, and make sure she met everybody. Now, it seemed, the thanks they were getting for their efforts was a slap in the face.

John-Boy made no attempt to talk to her. After the service, all of the Waltons lingered in front of the church talking to neighbors for about five minutes. But Amelia left almost immediately. Mary Ellen waved to her when she came down the steps. But Amelia gave her only a brief smile and strode off toward home.

It was possible, John-Boy guessed, that Amelia knew nothing about what was going on. But he really didn't believe it. After Mary Ellen waved, she certainly would have come over and talked to them.

Mary Ellen finished her dress during the afternoon. After her treatments, Olivia asked her to model it for all of them, and everyone, including John, came up to her room for the show. It would have been fun, John-Boy guessed, if it weren't for his black mood.

With everyone waiting, Mary Ellen took an extra five minutes to be sure everything was just right. Then, chin high and sliding sideways through the door, she made her grand entrance and twirled slowly around the room.

Jason struck a chord on his guitar. "And from the kingdom of Walton's Mountain," he announced solemnly, "Princess Mary Ellen, the most sought-after maiden in the entire empire."

Mary Ellen curtsied to her mother. "Your Highness," she murmured, and bowed to the others. "And your most gracious royal court."

They all clapped.

"Darling, it's beautiful!" Olivia exclaimed. "It's just gorgeous!"

"Almost as pretty as the girl inside of it," Grandpa smiled.

It was about the prettiest dress John-Boy could ever remember seeing. Mostly it was white, with some kind of lacy white material over the shinier cloth underneath. And the pink ribbon they had brought back from Charlottesville gave it just the right feminine touch.

John-Boy noticed that his father was smiling. But his eyes looked distant, as if he was thinking about other things.

"John-Boy, would you dance with Mary Ellen?" his mother asked, "Just for a minute. I'd love to see how her skirt sways with the music."

John-Boy made no protests this time. His mother was having a good time and he didn't want to ruin it. Jason struck a chord and sang "The Tennessee Waltz," and John-Boy bowed and lightly took Mary Ellen's hand.

Surprisingly, she moved smoothly, hardly resisting his movements at all. It was as if the dress had transformed her into a girl instead of a tomboy, and she suddenly had a natural grace. John-Boy twirled her slowly around, circling the room twice, and then broke away with another bow.

"That's marvelous," Grandma said and clapped. "I declare, I think you two should go down to Charlottesville and enter one of them waltzin contests."

Jason laughed. "That's all fine, but who's gonna teach G. W. how to dance?"

"I'll do it," Mary Ellen said firmly.

"Tell him you want to play some catch out in the woods," Erin suggested. "Then make him dance."

Mary Ellen stared at her. "Good idea," she nodded.

John-Boy couldn't help smiling. When she was dancing, Mary Ellen was as graceful and feminine as she could be. But when there was a job to be done, she was all business. John-Boy felt a little sorry for G. W.

In their lighthearted mood, no one else seemed to notice their father's silence. But suddenly he was on his feet, heading for the door. "I reckon I'd better get back to work," he said as he went out.

It caught everyone by surprise. After a minute, Grandpa glanced quickly at John-Boy and smiled. "I reckon your Daddy's right. We better be getten supper started. And get this house cleaned up."

"But we cleaned it yesterday," Jim-Bob protested.

"Yes, and I found a half pound of dust on the mantelpiece this mornen."

"And you'd better get that dress off," Grandma said. "I think we can still take in a little around the waist."

As they filed out, John-Boy saw that his mother was smiling at him. "John-Boy? Would you stay and tell me about what courses you've picked out to take?"

He stayed and took the chair next to her bed. "I haven't really picked out any courses yet, Mama. I haven't had much time to study the catalogue."

She nodded and looked off at the window. "John-Boy, what's botherin your father?"

The question took him by surprise. But the last thing he intended telling her was the truth. On the other hand, he couldn't think of anything reasonable to say in its place.

"I reckon he's just tired, Mama. He's been cutten an awful lot of wood lately."

"Wood cutten never made your Daddy tired."

"Well—I guess he's worried about you, too. Not worried—I mean concerned. I know he wants like anythen for you to get well as fast as possible."

She continued staring at the window. "You know, John-Boy, the first dance your daddy and I went to, I had a dress almost exactly like Mary Ellen's. I think your daddy might have been thinken about that. He might have been rememberen how we danced and danced. And I guess *laughed* about as much as we danced." She paused, and for a minute John-Boy was afraid she was going to cry. "You know, it's hard on your Daddy, John-Boy. It's hard for a man to see his wife like this. Sometimes I think it's harder on him than on me."

John-Boy swallowed hard. "But you're gonna get better, Mama. You're moven your legs a little bit. And even Dr. Miller said you're doen a lot better than he did when he first got sick."

She nodded, as if trying to convince herself. "Yes, I'm gonna get better, John-Boy. I'm goen to walk." She smiled anxiously at him. "Help your daddy, John-Boy. He's a strong man and he likes to solve all his problems by himself. But even he needs help sometimes."

"I will, Mama. I'll try."

After everyone said goodnight, John-Boy sat at his desk for a long time before he put anything in his notebook. When he did start writing, his pen was as heavy as his heart.

Easter is now less than a week away. I don't think Mama is going to walk to sunrise services. I sometimes wonder—and I think she does too—if she will ever walk again.

This is the worst winter we have ever had; the worst time we have ever had, and I wonder if there will ever be Spring. Grandma and Grandpa pray every night, and I think they truly believe there will be a miracle of some kind. Is there wisdom in their years? Or do they pray from desperation and despair?

IX

Going to school Monday morning, John-Boy felt that things could not possibly get any worse. Before he got home that afternoon he found that they could—a lot worse.

During classes he paid no attention to Amelia Claybourne, and her attitude toward him seemed to be one of complete indifference. John-Boy decided that if she knew about the theft and her mother's accusations, she either didn't care, or she was discreetly ignoring it. But at ten minutes past three that idea was quickly shattered.

Normally all the Walton children walked home together. Some occasionally lingered a few minutes to talk to Miss Hunter, or their friends. But the others waited, or walked slowly until the laggards caught up. But that afternoon, after waiting nearly ten minutes for Erin and Mary Ellen, they all headed back. Behind the school they found an angry shouting match—Amelia Claybourne and Martha Rose Coverdale against Erin and Mary Ellen. Erin was in tears.

"If you don't take it back," she screamed in a quivering voice, "my daddy'll come over with his rifle and make you! You're the biggest liar in all Jefferson County!"

"Hah!" Martha Rose sneered. "If anybody should take somethen back, it's your daddy. And I don't mean his dumb old rifle."

"He didn't steal anybody's silver goblets!" Mary Ellen shouted. "And you know it, Amelia!"

130

Amelia was trying her best to look smug and superior. "If you want the truth, Mary Ellen Walton, all you have to do is ask Sheriff Ep Bridges who took them."

"Liar!"

At the first mention of the goblets, John-Boy's heart sank. But he didn't know what to do or say about it. He stopped well short of the shouters. "Mary Ellen, Erin, come on!"

They turned sharply. "You know what Amelia Claybourne said, John-Boy?! She said—"

"I know. Now, come on. They don't know what they're talken about."

"You'll find out," Martha Rose said with a sickening sweet smile. "When you get home, just ask your daddy." With that, both she and Amelia turned away.

"I'll ask him to come over and whip you and your daddy, and your whole family," Mary Ellen shouted after them.

"Come on, Mary Ellen."

When he finally got them headed for home, John-Boy had no choice but to explain it. Even if he could have kept Erin and Mary Ellen quiet, the others had heard enough to demand answers.

He told them that Sheriff Bridges came two nights ago and told their father that two goblets were missing from the Claybournes' house. He knew very well that their father didn't take them, but because he was the only caller at the house, Mrs. Claybourne came to the dumb conclusion that he might have taken them. Anyhow, John-Boy said—hedging a little—Sheriff Bridges was just asking their father if he might have some idea where the goblets were.

"Then that's why Daddy's been acten so strange," Jason said.

"Yes. He was mad that Mrs. Claybourne would think he might have taken the things."

"I hate that old lady," Jim-Bob muttered.

"Me too!" Elizabeth said.

John-Boy nodded, at the same time trying to think.

He had to impress on them how important it was for their mother not to hear about it. And he had no idea what his father would do if he heard the story was being spread all over the place.

"Now listen—all of you. While there's not much reason to be thinken too favorably about the Claybournes right now, we all have to be as grown up about this as we can. We can't waste our time hatin people. And the most important thing is we can't let Mama hear about any of this. You understand?"

They all nodded glumly.

"But John-Boy, how can that woman say such a thing?"

"I don't know. Maybe she's getten old and crazy. But that's not important right now." He looked around at each of them. "Is there anyone here who thinks Daddy stole those goblets?"

"No!" they chorused.

"That's crazy!" Jason said.

"Of course it's crazy. We know it's crazy, and pretty soon everybody'll know it. So we just gotta be patient, and not get mad when people like Martha Rose and Amelia say things. We just gotta show 'em we're stronger and got more good sense than they have. And we do that by keepen our mouths shut."

John-Boy hoped he got the point across. All of them except Ben were nodding. He stumbled along with his hands in his pockets, frowning.

"Do you agree, Ben?"

"Yeah. But I was thinken about somethen."

"What?"

"Well, you know yesterday, when I went out to deliver some of my magazines, two of my customers canceled their subscriptions. They took the magazines I brought, but they said they didn't want any more. They said they couldn't afford it."

John-Boy's heart sank again. But if someone like Martha Rose Coverdale knew all about the accusations, he supposed everybody in Walton's Mountain knew—or would know soon enough.

"Maybe they were tellen the truth," John-Boy said, "Maybe they couldn't afford it."

"I don't think it was that. They acted real funny when they told me. Kind of unfriendly."

"When does Mrs. Claybourne say Daddy took the goblets, John-Boy?" Jason asked.

"A week ago last Friday."

"Huh," Mary Ellen grunted, "that was the day Daddy bought Mama the bedjacket. That's funny. Daddy was doen somethen nice, and that old—that lady, says he was out stealin her dumb silver."

John-Boy looked sharply at her, but said nothing. When they came within sight of the house, he smiled at each of them. "Now nobody lets on, OK? Especially with Mama, we're all gonna be cheerful."

They all nodded and fixed smiles on their faces.

John-Boy was relieved to see that the truck was gone. At least everyone would get some practice at being cheerful before their father got home.

Ep Bridges spent most of the morning at the Claybournes'. But for all the good it did, he might just as well have stayed at home. Mrs. Claybourne claimed that all their searching of the house turned up the fact that nine more pieces of silver were missing.

"And they're very precious pieces, Sheriff. Not the ordinary ones I use every day."

"Well, Mrs. Claybourne, I'd say that should give you even less reason for suspecten John Walton. I don't see how he could of walked out of here with eleven pieces without anybody seein' him. A man'd need a suitcase for that kind of load."

"Not if he made two trips, Sheriff. And that's exactly what Mr. Walton did. After his first visit, he claimed he had to come back because the refrigerator needed a new part. And we have no way of knowing if that was true, do we? It could simply have been an excuse to get back in the house again."

"I talked to Ike Godsey, Mrs. Claybourne. A new

part was ordered for your refrigerator, and John picked it up."

"That only proves to me that he planned the whole thing very carefully. Apparently it was not an impulsive act after all."

Sheriff Bridges felt a little sick. He was sitting in the Claybournes' fancy house, sipping coffee from little cups that probably cost ten dollars each, and this "grand" lady was slandering a man who had more integrity in his little finger than she had in her whole family. He put the cup down, wiped his hands on the linen napkin and tossed it on the table.

"Mrs. Claybourne, John Walton is not your man. I want you once and for all to simply take my word for that."

"I am aware of the fact that he is your friend, Sheriff Bridges, and I understand your loyalty to him. But you see, there simply hasn't been anyone else here."

Ep nodded and rose. "You're gonna need more evidence than that before I can put a man under arrest, ma'am."

"Then what am I to do? Simply stand by while all my good silver vanishes into thin air?"

"For the time bein', I'd suggest you put it all under lock and key."

"That's well and good, Mr. Bridges. But that doesn't bring back what's already been stolen."

Ep's feeling of depression wasn't helped any when he walked into Ike Godsey's an hour later. He had hoped to have a short, friendly game of pool so he could mull over some things in his mind. But the only person in the store besides Ike was Dodge Evenhauer, and he was knocking pool balls around waiting for someone to play with.

If there was one man in all of Walton's Mountain who would have a hard time finding someone to loan him a nickel, Ep guessed it would be Dodge Evenhauer. Dodge was about thirty-five, and a decent enough-looking man. But because he had never amounted to much himself, he was always working hard at pointing out the faults of everyone else in Walton's Mountain.

Ike was totaling up accounts behind his counter when Ep came in. "Hey, Ep." He winked and tossed his head toward the rear of the store. "Dodge Evenhauer's back there wanten a game."

Ep nodded wearily and headed back.

"Hey, looken for some competition, Sheriff? Shoot you some eight-ball for fifty cents."

"Gamblen on pool's against the law, Dodge."

Sheriff Bridges would have had a hard time counting all the pool games he'd played for money. But those were all with honest men. With Dodge Evenhauer, the only contest was seeing how many times you could catch him cheating.

"OK," Dodge smiled, "then just for fun?"

Ep nodded and got a cue. "Go ahead and break 'em."

Dodge racked up the balls and gave them a hard break, but none dropped. Ep lined up a shot and eased the cue slowly back.

"Well, how's it feel, Sheriff, to find out that our local man who can do no wrong ain't no different from the rest of us?"

Ep took a minute to steady his cue again. He shot and missed. "What're you blatherin about, Dodge?"

Dodge grinned and curled over the table. "Well, who'd've thought good old upstanden John Walton would end up on the wrong side of the law?"

Ep felt his stomach turn sour. "Dodge, did you know Olivia Walton's got polio?"

"Yeah, that's too bad. You figure that's a good enough reason for John to be stealen stuff?" Dodge smiled and circled the table for another shot.

"Dodge, I'd strongly recommend you just keep your mouth shut on things you don't know nothen about."

Dodge dropped another ball. "You don't have to get so touchy, Sheriff. It's pretty common knowledge around. And it don't look like you got no other suspects. Don't see why you're holden back on arresten him. Course now he's your friend, ain't he."

Ep nodded and watched him make another shot. "As I recall, Dodge, you get your firewood from John Walton."

"Yeah. So what?"

Dodge finally missed. Ep moved around the table and lined up a shot. "You wouldn't happen to be a little behind in payen him, would you?"

"Well, now, I reckon everybody owes somebody these days, Sheriff."

Ep made a smooth bank shot. He straightened and gave Dodge a cool smile. "That's true enough, Dodge. But not everybody's so quick to look for a way never to have to pay up."

Dodge seemed to have no answer for that. He finally grinned and shrugged. Then they both looked up as the bell tinkled on Ike's door. Ep smiled to himself and lined up another shot. It was John Walton.

He heard Ike and John's greetings, but they were short. Then John was standing in the pool room, a determined look on his face.

"Dodge, I saw your flivver parked out front. I been callen around on all my owin customers. Your bill's four dollars, and you've owed since November."

Ep glanced over at Dodge. But the man was suddenly cocky again.

"Well, John," he smiled, "Maybe I should just send the money on to your lawyer."

The movement came fast. But the angry twitch in John Walton's mouth was warning enough, and Ep got between them. He caught the wrist at the same moment John's hand clamped onto Dodge's shirt front. Dodge Evenhauer was lucky. If John Walton had thrown a punch, there would have been no way for Ep to stop it.

"Take it easy, John," Ep said.

There was a tense moment when Ep wasn't sure

what was going to happen. Then the hand came off the shirt and Dodge backed away, his face pale.

"Dodge," Ep said, "Maybe it's you who better be getten a lawyer. Not payen your debts is against the law, too. Now get out of here and get on with your business."

Dodge stood for a minute, as if groping for some kind of a face-saving remark. Then he scooped up his jacket and strode away.

"I should have hit him," John muttered when the door finally banged shut.

"That man ain't worth skinnin your knuckles on, John." Ep moved slowly around the table retrieving balls from the pockets. "John, I got a phone call early this mornen. Seems like you was seen in Charlottesville the day you fixed the Claybournes' refrigerator."

"Is that against the law?"

"No. And don't take me wrong. I still ain't sayen you stole nothen." Ep put his pool cue in the rack. The whole situation was delicate, and he didn't want to get John's blood boiling again. But he'd also like some information. "John, in times like these a man sometimes has to do things he never thought he'd do under other circumstances. And a man's family comes first. If I had a wife who was sick—well—I can see myself having to—I can see myself bein' tempted."

Ep didn't expect any sudden confession from John Walton. But he thought this might at least soften him up a little. The last thing he expected was the easy smile that came to John's face.

"That's a funny thing for you to say, Ep. Because, frankly, I can't see you bein' tempted by anythen."

It took Ep a minute to digest the statement. But that time, John Walton was already passing by Ike and going out the front door. But Ep continued staring after him, wondering—certain now that he was right in what he had told Mrs. Claybourne.

But damn it, he thought, that still didn't tell him who took all that silver.

Mary Ellen's remark about their father having come home with the new bedjacket the same day the silver was supposedly stolen had given John-Boy's memory an unpleasant jolt. There had been more than a new bedjacket. That was also the day the truck suddenly had two new tires.

"You sell some firewood, Daddy?"

John-Boy distinctly remembered Jason's question. But what had his father answered? It was something about the Claybournes. He had said, "No, but I got the Claybournes' refrigerator fixed."

What did that mean? It really meant nothing. If the Claybournes had paid him enough to buy the tires and the bedjacket, he would have said so. Wouldn't he?

John-Boy wrestled with the questions all through the afternoon and past supper. Of all the children, he guessed he was the least successful at maintaining a cheerful face in front of his mother. But she didn't seem to notice.

G. W. Haines made an appearance late in the day and stayed for supper. Nothing was mentioned about the Claybournes' missing silver, but John-Boy had the feeling G. W.'s visit was his way of showing the Waltons he was on their side. John-Boy felt grateful.

After G. W. went home and all the paraphernalia from their mother's treatment was cleaned up, John-Boy wandered out to the barn. For awhile he watched Chance munching quietly in her feed bin. Then he moved to the barn window and gazed out at the mountains.

It was a chilly, moonlit night. A scattering of high clouds drifted silently across the sky, and their shadows made big blotches that slowly crept up and slid past the tops of the hills. Farther away, the mountains seemed to have a phosphorescent lining along their ridges.

John-Boy had an ominous feeling about how things were going to turn out.

His father certainly couldn't have taken that silver.

But where did he get the money for the tires and the bedjacket? Had he made some collections from people who owed him for firewood? Or, maybe, had he won it in a poker game and he was ashamed to admit it? John-Boy had heard stories about big poker games going on down in Charlottesville. But his father couldn't have been down there more than an hour or two.

Why did all this have to happen now, John-Boy wondered miserably. Everybody couldn't keep slinking around trying to keep it a secret from their mother forever. And he was already having doubts about her recovery. It was possible, he was now coming to realize, that they could go on and on with the treatments, only to have her legs finally wither away into lifeless stumps. There was no God looking after them, and there was no immutable law of justice that guaranteed any reward in return for their mother's persistence and suffering.

John-Boy leaned heavily on the window sill and closed his eyes, trying to deny this conclusion. If she didn't recover, he had the dark feeling that the whole family might be doomed far worse than the misfortune of his mother being crippled. It seemed like there were already signs of it.

"John-Boy?"

The voice was soft, and almost directly behind him. He turned sharply.

His father must have been standing there for some time. His hands were in his back pockets and he was gazing distantly through the window.

"Hi, Daddy."

His father moved up and leaned on the sill. "Pretty night."

"Yes, it is."

His father took a deep breath and looked at his hands. "I shouldn't have sent you in the house the other night."

His father's harsh command that night hadn't really bothered John-Boy that much. He knew the anger was mostly directed at Sheriff Bridges. "I trust you, Daddy. And I believe in you. But—but sometimes I'm not even sure you want me to."

"I didn't take the Claybournes' silver, John-Boy."

"You know I didn't think that, Daddy. But it's—it's as if you don't trust me the way I do you."

"I'm sorry, John-Boy. I know it looks that way. But I did somethen—somethen I'm not too proud of."

"Then why can't you trust me? If somethen was botheren me, you'd expect me to tell you about it."

His father gazed at the mountains for a long time. "It doesn't directly concern you, John-Boy. It doesn't concern anybody but me—and one other person. And that person doesn't even know about it."

John-Boy felt a flash of anger. His father was talking in riddles, paying no attention to what he had been trying to tell him. But he quickly choked off any responses, remembering his mother's anxious words. "Help your daddy, John-Boy. He's a strong man and he likes to solve all his problems by himself. But even he needs help sometimes."

"Daddy, I don't think I know what you're talken about. But I'll do anythen in the world you want me to. I guess I love you and Mama so much—so much I can't even say it in words. And I want to help."

There were suddenly tears standing in his father's eyes. "John-Boy, there's nothen you can do any more than you've just done. What you've said means a whole lot to me."

They stood for a long time, John-Boy wishing he could think of something more to say—or that his father would tell him something to do. His father finally sighed heavily. He put a hand on John-Boy's shoulder, then moved away.

"Better be comen up pretty soon, son."

Dr. Vance came late the next afternoon. He spent almost an hour upstairs. When he came down he accepted a cup of coffee, and everyone except Olivia and Erin gathered at the kitchen table.

"So far, the removal of the splints appears to have caused no damage," he said. "But it may be too early to tell. Unfortunately, there also appears to be no change in her reflexes. In light of that, I'm afraid I'm not optimistic."

"But Livvy says she's got some feelen in the legs now," John protested, "A lot more than a week ago."

Dr. Vance nodded. "That may mean nothing, Mr. Walton. Our sensory nerves can very easily deceive us. Many times people who lose a hand or a leg still have the sensation of feeling, as if they still had the limb. I'm inclined to think that is what your wife is experiencing."

"But how about the movement?" Grandpa said, "Sometimes Livvy can turn her ankles or lift her knees right up off the bed. We've seen it."

John-Boy knew the statement was only partially true. She had moved her ankles and knees. But just as often he had seen her struggle painfully with no results at all.

"We have to be careful about drawing any conclusions," Dr. Vance said. "If they are not totally destroyed, some of the nerves will recover to a certain degree. That generally happens with all polio patients. But you should understand, the recovery will be limited by the extent of the nerve damage. In other words, her progress could come to a complete standstill at any time."

"But that doesn't mean we shouldn't keep on tryen," Grandma said defiantly.

Dr. Vance gazed solemnly across the table at John. "From what I can tell, it's still not too late to put the leg braces back on, Mr. Walton. The worst possible damage can still be avoided. And I noticed a fine looking wheelchair standing in the hall up there."

"Mama doesn't want to use a wheelchair!" John-Boy almost screamed. He was as surprised as everybody else by the anger in his words.

"That's right," his father said more calmly, "I don't

think Livvy'll even consider it until she's tried every-then else. And I agree with her."

Dr. Vance nodded thoughtfully. He seemed to come to some kind of decision, and brought some papers from his pocket. "I've been aware of your decision, of course. And I suspected that no matter what I said today you wouldn't change it. With that in mind, and thinking that as long as you're going to continue the treatments, I had Dr. Pierce wire this woman in Australia."

"Sister Kenny!?"

"Yes. It occurred to me that her techniques might have advanced some since those brochures were print-ed. In any case, here's what she sent." Dr. Vance smiled, aware of the shocked reaction his contradic-tory actions had created.

"Doc," John said, "that's awful nice of you to go to all that trouble."

"And we appreciate it," Grandma added.

Dr. Vance rose and got his bag. "Well, if you're going to do something, I guess you should do it ex-actly the way you're supposed to."

John got quickly to his feet. "I'll see you out to your car."

Dr. Vance was parked in front. As they passed through the living room and out the front door, John realized that up until a couple of minutes ago he had not liked Dr. Vance very much. From that moment two weeks ago when the doctor told him to sit down, and then announced that Olivia had polio, it had seemed like Dr. Vance's only interest in Olivia was to get her into braces and a wheelchair as quickly as pos-sible. But it was clear enough now that he was not as stubborn and narrow-minded as he appeared.

"Doc," John said when they reached the car, "I think maybe I owe you an apology. Your senden off for those instructions was a generous thing to do."

Dr. Vance nodded as if he had been fully aware of the antagonism. "We all make mistakes, Mr. Walton," he said quietly. "And maybe I was wrong." He put his bag in the car, but stood for a minute, frowning thoughtfully. "I'm concerned about your wife. But I'll confess, I'm also a little puzzled."

"How so?"

"There are a lot of unusual aspects to her case. In fact, I talked to Dr. Miller at Boatwright College the other day, and he agreed with me. For one thing, her being able to sit up so quickly after the initial sickness. Generally, the attack is so severe the patient is left almost totally helpless for a considerable length of time."

"You mean it's possible she doesn't have polio?"

"No, I don't think there's any question about her having had the disease. But it could be a matter of degree. It's like any other disease—some people's natural defenses fight off the invasions more successfully. It is possible, and there have been instances like this, where the attack on the nervous system stopped just short of doing permanent damage. Such cases are rare, but they happen."

"But wouldn't she be better by now?"

"Not necessarily. The attack could still have been severe enough that it would take some time for the nerves to recover. It's like getting a hard blow on an arm or leg. The bones might not be broken, or the ligaments torn. But the muscles could be so bruised and swollen the limb would still be useless. In that case the recovery would be only a matter of time."

John's hopes rose cautiously. My God, he thought, what wouldn't he do to have Olivia be one of those rare cases.

"It's hard to know what is the right thing to do," Dr. Vance went on, "If the nerves are destroyed—and in most instances this is the case—then the best thing is to put the splints back on and protect the limbs from excessive deformity. If the nerves are not destroyed, it still wouldn't hurt to have the splints on. That's why I feel it would be the safest procedure. On the other hand, if the nerves aren't destroyed, the Sister Kenny treatment won't hurt either. In fact it would probably be good for her."

"But there's no way of telling for certain if the nerves have been destroyed?"

Dr. Vance thought a minute and shook his head. "Perhaps in a hospital more delicate tests could be made. But even then it would be hard to tell if a nerve is really dead, or only temporarily numbed. No, I think it's a matter of time, Mr. Walton. And maybe prayer. But what we'll be praying for is something that's already happened." He smiled. "I guess it's like waiting for the results of a baseball game that was played two weeks ago. We're not praying for them to win, but to hear that they won."

"You mean what we do now won't make any difference?"

"It'll make a great deal of difference if she was lucky two weeks ago. If the nerves are still alive, I think the Sister Kenny treatments will help them come out of shock, so to speak." He got in the car and smiled. "I'm going to pray that she was lucky."

John watched him drive off—uncertain if he was encouraged, or more depressed than before. They were gambling. And from what Dr. Vance said, the odds were heavily against them. But for the sake of everyone else in the family, John could see no other choice but to gamble that Olivia had won.

The papers the doctor had left contained detailed instructions for the massaging of the legs, along with day-by-day schedules for heat applications. Altogether, they were not a great deal different from what they were doing already. But they swept away any doubts, and gave everyone a new sense of determination.

Although no one mentioned the subject out loud, it was clear that everybody at school knew about Mrs. Claybourne's accusations. What relieved John-Boy was that almost everyone seemed to be on their side. "That Amelia Claybourne is stupid," kids would remark casually. Or, "Martha Rose Coverdale is over there shooten off her big mouth again."

These indirect expressions of support were reassuring for the Waltons. But they still didn't solve the problem. And what made it worse, the only place they could discuss it with any freedom was walking to and from school.

"What're we gonna do, John-Boy?"

"I don't know. I reckon we'll just have to wait till Sheriff Bridges finds out what happened to the silver."

"What if he never finds out?"

That was the worst thing that could happen, and the question that nagged at John-Boy.

"If you ask me," Jim-Bob said, "the Claybournes probably got all that silver hidden in their basement or something."

"Why would they do that?"

"I don't know."

"Because they're mean," Elizabeth said.

"Nobody'd be that mean."

"Amelia would," Erin said. "I wish she'd never come to our school. Why didn't she just stay in her old fancy private school down in Richmond?"

"They probably kicked her out." Jason muttered.

"Yeah, she's so dumb," Ben added.

It was odd, John-Boy reflected, that the Claybournes had taken Amelia out of private school, particularly in the middle of the school year. That might be something to think about.

X

"I don't know, John-Boy. I'm not sure I can go through with this."

"Why not? It'll only take a minute. C'mon, Ben, we gotta do somethen to try and help Daddy."

"They're probably not even home."

John-Boy gave Ben an impatient look. It was obvious there was someone home—at least Stuart Lee. His roadster was parked right at the top of the driveway.

They had approached the house from the far side, where the woods came to the edge of the big circular driveway. From there they had crept through the shrubs almost to the corner of the house, and then ducked behind a low hedge.

John-Boy had proposed the idea to Ben early in the morning, before they left for school. The more John-Boy thought about it, the stranger it seemed—if the Claybournes were so all-fired rich and snooty, why had they taken their only daughter out of private school? The only conclusion that made any sense, was that maybe the Claybournes weren't so all-fired rich. Maybe, like everyone else in the world these days, they were having money problems. If that was so, maybe it had something to do with the disappearance of the silver.

"You mean you think they stole it themselves?" Ben had asked.

"I don't know. Maybe they've got insurance on it, or somethen."

"Well, if they're so poor, how could they buy insurance?"

John-Boy hadn't considered that. But he still thought it was a good idea to find out just how rich or poor they were. And if Ben went to their door and tried to sell them some magazine subscriptions, maybe he could just find out.

Ben had no faith in the plan at all. But he agreed to take his canvas bag and a few magazines to school. From there they went directly to the Claybournes'.

"The worst thing that can happen," John-Boy told him now, "is that they'll just say no."

"What good will that do us? They could still be the richest people in the world and say no. In fact with them thinken Daddy took their stupid silver they'll probably throw me down the porch steps."

"They won't do that."

Ben wasn't so sure. He gazed silently through the hedge and up at the big house, his heart already beginning to pound against his ribs. He knew very well it wasn't going to work. He and John-Boy were crazy to come within five miles of this place.

He looked at the yellow roadster parked in front, then at the steps, and finally at the big front door. He also knew very well that John-Boy would stand here in the mud forever before he would let him go home. Ben took a deep breath and rose. "OK," he said unsteadily.

Once he straightened, he adjusted the bag on his shoulder and made sure there was a magazine ready to pull out. He took another long breath, stepped out from behind the hedge and marched steadily forward.

At the door he pressed the electric bell, and then out of nervousness he pounded the big brass knocker. As quickly as he did it he wished he hadn't. It sounded like there was someone angry and impatient at the door.

When the door opened, Ben's heart almost stopped beating. The worst person possible was standing there—Amelia.

"Well!" she said.

"Uh—hi. I'd like to see your brother, please."

She looked surpirsed, as if she didn't know what to do for a minute. But she opened the door a little wider and Ben moved quickly inside.

"What do you want to see him about?"

Ben opened his mouth to answer, but found himself gaping at the big staircase, his heart racing wildly. Mrs. Claybourne was coming down, glaring coldly at him.

"Amelia—go to your room, please."

Amelia shrugged and moved off. Ben stood paralyzed as the woman came toward him.

"Young man, I think it is inappropriate for you to appear at this house under the present circumstances."

Ben had no idea how to respond. Then words were tumbling breathlessly from his mouth. "Mrs. Claybourne, I'm here to offer you a unique opportunity. A very small group of people in our community has been selected to—"

"I'm afraid you didn't hear me correctly, young man! I think you had better—"

"But ma'am, I represent four of the finest periodicals now bein' published in this country, and for a limited time only—"

"Stuart Lee? Stuart Lee, please come in here." Mrs. Claybourne moved to a big open door at the side. Stuart Lee appeared as quickly as she got there.

"What is it, Mama?" He saw Ben and smiled. "Hello, Ben."

"Son, would you please explain to this child that he is not welcome here until the situation concerning his family is cleared up?"

Ben had an urge to turn and bolt through the front door, but his legs were quivering too much for him to trust them. Stuart Lee looked embarrassed.

"I'll talk to Ben, Mama."

"I knew you'd take care of it, dear." Mrs. Claybourne smiled and continued through the door.

"I'm sorry, Ben. My mother is a little upset today."

"That's OK." Ben suddenly remembered that he hadn't pulled a magazine from his bag. He slid one out. "I just came because of this unique opportunity I have to offer. You see, for a limited time, I'm able to make an exceptional offer. It's four magazines for five dollars. Delivered right here to your door."

Stuart Lee glanced at the magazine. "Ben, I don't think this is a good time to talk business." He moved toward the front door. "Thank you for the opportunity, but we really can't afford—we really don't need any magazines."

Ben stared at him, his heart now almost leaping into his mouth. John-Boy was right! It was exactly as he said. Stuart Lee almost said they couldn't afford to buy any magazines, but then caught himself and changed it. Ben stared incredulously, looking at Stuart Lee from head to foot. The door was now open and Stuart Lee was smiling at him. Ben edged past, putting the magazine away. "Well, thank you very much, Stuart Lee."

"You're welcome, Ben."

As quickly as he heard the door close behind him, Ben bounded down the stairs and raced past John-Boy. "C'mon, John-Boy, let's get out of here!"

They retraced their course through the shrubbery and were back in the woods before John-Boy caught up with him.

"It was awful, John-Boy. But you were right. Stuart Lee said they couldn't afford any magazines. Then he changed it, like he didn't mean to say that. Mrs. Claybourne acted like I was some kind of criminal. She kept goen on about Daddy takin the silver. and everythen."

"I'm sorry, Ben. I shouldn't have made you do it."

"It's OK. And I noticed somethen else, John-Boy. But promise you won't laugh when I tell you."

"What?"

They were a safe distance away now and Ben stopped. He glanced back at the big house. "Well, it's like somethen I saw in a Charlie Chan movie. Number

One Son said you can always tell when a rich man is just pretenden to have money and he really doesn't."

"What about it?"

"It's their shoes."

"Their shoes?" John-Boy laughed.

"I know it sounds funny. But the movie said that after rich people lose their money their shoes look bad—like they need fixen. And you know somethen? The Claybournes have got shoes with the heels run over."

"All of 'em?"

"Well, I don't know about Mrs. Claybourne. She was wearin one of them long, bedroom-like dresses. But Stuart Lee's shoes looked terrible. And I remember at school today, so did Amelia's. I thought they were just old shoes for playen or somethen, but I don't know."

John-Boy shook his head, thinking. "Ben, I think you've been seein' too many movies. But maybe you've got somethen."

John-Boy had even less enthusiasm for carrying out the second part of his investigation. But he needed more substantial information than the fact that the Claybournes wore old shoes and wouldn't buy a magazine subscription. And getting that kind of information might not be so easy. Halfway home, John-Boy left Ben and headed for Ike Godsey's.

There were no customers in the store. Ike was opening a fresh bag of coffee beans, scooping them into the bin next to the grinder.

"Hey, John-Boy, what can I do for you?"

"Oh, nothen, Ike. Just thought I'd stop by to see if we got any mail."

"Nope. Your daddy checked earlier."

"Can I give you a hand?"

Ike smiled and set the scoop aside. "I'd be obliged, John-Boy. If you can pick up the sack, I'll guide the beans in here."

John-Boy lifted the sack and the beans rattled down into the bin.

"How's business, Ike?"

"Oh, not too bad. Be a lot better if people could pay their bills."

John-Boy smiled. Ike couldn't have given him a better opening. "I reckon just about everybody buys their stuff on credit nowadays, huh?"

"That's the truth."

Ike went back into his storeroom and John-Boy followed, keeping his voice casual. "Does anybody pay cash at all anymore?"

"Ike laughed. "About the only ones are the kids. For little things, like candy. But for food and necessities, about everybody charges."

"Huh," John-Boy said and helped Ike carry out sacks of flour. "Even rich people like the Claybournes charge stuff, I suppose."

"Oh, yeah."

"But I reckon they pay up right smart at the end of the month."

Ike gave him a wary glance. "Well, now, John-Boy, it ain't exactly ethical for me to be talken about how my customers pay their bills." He chuckled. "But I reckon a depression hits rich and poor people all alike."

John-Boy figured he'd better not pursue that too directly. "Where'd the Claybournes get all their money in the first place, Ike?"

"Oh, I reckon it's just been in the family for years. And after Carter died there was some insurance money. But they ran through that pretty fast. I reckon rich people get some fancy spenden habits and they're hard to break."

John-Boy felt his pulse quicken, but he shrugged easily. "So they're just broke like everybody else, huh?"

"Well, in some ways I reckon they're even worse off, John-Boy. Us poor folks have pretty much always been maken do with nothen. For them, they

don't know how. Why, Stuart Lee still comes in here
and buys those fancy tinned English cookies for his
mother. They cost a dollar, and your Grandma could
make twice as many that would taste twice as good
for about twenty cents. Now if they'd settle up their
bill, it wouldn't make no difference to me one way or
the other. But I'll tell you, John-Boy, I only got three
of those tins left, and I been thinken of hidin 'em before Stuart Lee comes in here again."

John-Boy couldn't imagine a clearer statement of
the Claybournes' financial situation. "That's too bad,"
he said and looked over at Ike's clock. "Gee, is it almost five o'clock? I gotta get goen, Ike."

"OK. And thanks for the help, John-Boy."

Walking home, John-Boy felt that the matter was
settled—the Claybournes were as short of money as
anybody else. Maybe worse off. But as significant as
that might be, it still didn't solve the problem. Being
broke was no good reason for them to accuse his father of stealing. John-Boy had felt elated by the results of his and Ben's detective work. But now the excitement was gone. The question still needed a lot of
thought. John-Boy shoved his hands deep into his
pockets and tried to arrange all the facts into some
sensible pattern.

At exactly seven-thirty that night, there was a hesi-
tant knock on the Waltons' front door. The others
were in the kitchen, or upstairs, and John rose from
the sofa and answered it. As quickly as he opened the
door an amused smile came to his face.

Normally, G. W. Haines' arrival at the Walton
house came in the form a head appearing just inside
the back door, with G. W. asking if it was OK to
come in. Tonight he was wearing a dark suit that appeared to be a little baggy from being cut down to
fit. He was also wearing a polka-dot bow tie. His hair
was slick and shiny, and he was holding a paper sack
gingerly in front of him.

"Hey, G. W., you're looken slick as a city dude. C'mon in."

"Thank you, Mr. Walton. Is Mary Ellen ready?"

John closed the door and motioned to the sofa. "She oughta be down any minute. Have a seat. What's in the bag?"

"Oh, it's nothen, just a corsage. My Grandma made if for me—I mean for Mary Ellen."

John knew there were half a dozen people peeking out from the kitchen. It had been decided that they wouldn't sit around the living room and embarrass G. W. when he came. But Elizabeth suddenly hurried into the room.

"I'll take it up to her if you want, G. W."

"Yeah. Gee, thanks, Elizabeth."

G. W. appeared to be relieved to get rid of the bag. But he still didn't look too comfortable as he eased down on the edge of the sofa. John was sympathetic. On his first date with a girl he'd walked into a house full of strangers who spent ten minutes studying him from head to toe. At least G. W. was among friends.

"I see you got your dancen shoes on, G. W."

He moved his feet back a little. "Yes, sir."

"You and Mary Ellen been practicen?"

"No. Well—yes, some, I guess." G .W. shifted and smiled sheepishly. "I mean we were gonna play some catch yesterday out in the—in a clearin over yonder. But Mary Ellen had this old movie magazine. It had pictures of a guy named Fred Astaire, and some woman."

"Ginger Rogers?"

"Yeah."

John nodded, wishing he could have seen that. When Mary Ellen set out to learn something, at least she learned from the best.

"I think I've sort of got the hang of it," G. W. said. He grinned, and then leaped to his feet as he glanced at the stairs.

Mary Ellen was coming down slowly, smiling, delicately lifting her long skirt to keep from tripping.

The corsage of yellow flowers was pinned to the right side of her dress.

"Gee," G. W. said. "Gee, you really look good, Mary Ellen."

"Your corsage is just beautiful, G. W. I never even had a corsage before."

Until this moment John had paid little attention to Mary Ellen's dressmaking or dance lessons. But now a lump suddenly formed in his throat as he gazed at her. Mary Ellen was always the one with the smudged face and torn pants and baseball mitt jammed into her rear pocket. But the girl standing before him was a beautiful young lady. John was amazed—and even more amazed at himself for not realizing how remarkably pretty she was.

Everyone in the kitchen now came into the room. G. W. shoved his hands into his pockets and grinned, looking from the crowd to Mary Ellen.

"G. W.," John said, "If you wouldn't mind goen up, Mrs. Walton'd sure like to have a look at you two together."

"Sure. Be glad to, Mr. Walton."

John went up with them. He held the door open, and Mary Ellen came in first. She twirled lightly around and held her hand out for G. W.

"What do you think, Mama?"

John found himself grinning as he looked at Olivia. She looked like she was going to burst into joyful tears. She looked from one to the other, biting her lip. "Your sash is crooked," she finally said. "Let me straighten it for you."

Mary Ellen's sash was not crooked at all. But John knew Olivia was going to explode with pride and love if she didn't do something. She moved the sash back and forth an inch or two and then smiled, satisfied. "There! Mary Ellen, you're goen to be the prettiest girl there. And that corsage is beautiful, G .W."

"Thanks. My grandma made it."

Mary Ellen came back with her hand out. "Come on, G. W., let's show Mama how we dance."

G. W. stiffened. "Gee, Mary Ellen—"

"G. W.!"

John smiled and eased into a chair. He suspected that if this romance was going to continue, G. W. was either going to have to stand up more firmly for his convictions, or Mary Ellen was going to have to develop a little more tact. But right now, her command went unchallenged. G. W. obediently took her hand and they moved around the floor. It was hard to tell which of them was doing the leading.

Olivia was delighted. "John—aren't they good?"

"Very good. They remind me a lot of that couple who dance in the movies."

Mary Ellen brightened. "Fred Astaire and Ginger Rogers?"

"Yes, those are the ones."

"Gee, Daddy, really?"

John shrugged. "The only difference I can see is Fred Astaire wears a top hat."

"Did you hear that, G. W.?"

G. W. nodded and gave John a sly smile.

Mary Ellen took his hand. "Well, I reckon we'd better get goen, G. W. Bye, Mama, bye, Daddy."

"Have a wonderful time," Olivia called after them.

When they were gone John grinned at Olivia. But her head was back on the pillows, a dreamy smile on her face.

He went to the window and watched as G. W. helped Mary Ellen into the Haines' old Model T. After they drove off he found Olivia smiling suspiciously at him.

"John, you knew Mary Ellen had that old movie magazine, didn't you."

"What old movie magazine?" John tried, but he couldn't keep a straight face. "Yes, I heard somethen about it."

She laughed. "It was a nice thing to say, anyhow. I think it gave her a little more confidence in G. W. She did look beautiful, don't you think?"

John smiled to himself, thinking how beautiful she

did look. He moved to the chair next to the bed and took Olivia's hand as he sat down. "Yes, she did. In fact I'd say Mary Ellen was about the second most beautiful girl I've ever seen in my life."

Olivia smiled and looked up at him, waiting. He kissed her. Then she eased back and gazed reflectively at the ceiling.

"I remember the first dance I ever went to. It was terrible." She laughed. "I don't think the boy even knew what a dance was. He was wearen boots that must have weighed ten pounds each. But I guess it didn't matter. He spent the whole night staren at the dancers—as if all that swingen around was the craziest thing he'd ever seen in his life. I do hope that doesn't happen to Mary Ellen."

"I don't think there's much chance of that. If she wants G. W. to dance, he'll dance."

"I know. And I think maybe that's what I'm worried about. I do want Mary Ellen to realize she's a young lady instead of a baseball player. And enjoy bein' a young lady."

"Well, she seemed to enjoy bein' dressed up like one. I reckon the other things'll come along in time. And looken so much like her mother, there'll be lots of boys around reminden her she's a pretty girl."

Olivia smiled, pleased by the compliment, and by his confidence in Mary Ellen's future. John, in his refusal to worry about such things, was generally right.

"John?"

"What?"

"Would you carry me over to that chair by the window?"

"You sure you want to do that?"

She nodded. "I'd love to get out of this bed for awhile. And you could just prop my legs on another chair."

John studied her for a minute and then cautiously slid his arms under her. "If anythen hurts, let me know."

"I will."

As he lifted, her legs bent at the knees and she gasped for an instant. "It's all right," she assured him, and he carried her across to the chair. He quickly pulled another chair in place and lifted her feet to it. Once she was comfortable he got the quilt from the bed and wrapped it around her.

"Now you could bring over another chair, and turn out the lights."

John laughed. "What d'you have in mind, Livvy?"

"Nothen. I'd just like to sit with you, and look out at the night."

He brought over another chair and turned out the lights. When he sat down she took his hand again.

A silver moon stood high over Walton's Mountain. Around it, the mass of stars looked almost artificial in their brilliance. For a minute John reflected on the last time he had gazed out at those same stars—the night with John-Boy in the barn.

"You know," Olivia said softly, "I think I do worry about the children too much. Especially now. But I don't want them to waste time worryen about me. If the treatments don't work—"

"They're goen to work, Livvy."

She was silent for a minute. "But if they don't work—I mean, it's possible they won't. And I should be prepared to use that wheelchair—to spend the rest of my life in it. I think I can face that, John."

He didn't know how to respond. The possibility that the treatments wouldn't work had been weighing too heavily on his own mind. He gently squeezed her hand.

"But if that happens," she went on, "I don't want any of the children to feel they have to change their lives because of it. I think that's the worst thing they could do. You won't let that happen, will you, John?"

"No."

"But the worst part—the thing I dread most of all—is for you to have a crippled wife."

He looked sharply at her.

"No, I mean it, John. Thinken about that is worse for me than any of the pains in my legs."

"Just quit thinken about it, Livvy." He laughed. "We been married now almost twenty years, and I'd say I already got about three times more enjoyment out of those years than most men get out of sixty. And the fact is, no matter what happens with the treatments, I intend to keep on enjoyen bein' your husband."

She smiled and brushed her fingers across the back of his hand. "But I know it's affected you—my bein' sick. Especially in the last week." She smiled. "And I can understand why. It's hard enough supporten a family these days, without havin' me to take care of. But even if I have to use a wheelchair, I'll be able to help some. In fact, I been thinken about it. There's really lots of things I'll be able to do."

John frowned at her. "What do you mean, you've noticed it's affected me in the last week?"

"Well, you've been grumblen around like an old bear. You've been short with the children, you've hardly talked to me, or Grandma and Grandpa, and—"

"Livvy, darlin', that's got nothen to do with you. Not directly." He drew his hand away and rubbed his face, suddenly smiling. "Believe me, Livvy, it's not you bein' sick. It's—it's somethen else."

"What?"

He shook his head and looked out the window. "Livvy, about two weeks ago I did somethen I don't think I should have done—somethen I regretted very much about as quick as I did it. But—well, I'm not so sure now it was really as bad as I thought it was. I mean it's somethen that seemed important. But when you get right down to it, it really isn't. There's a lot more important things. I think I realized that tonight seein' Mary Ellen all grown up and goen off to dances."

Olivia stared at him. Then she couldn't help laughing. "John Walton, I've always thought of you as a man who came right to the point and said exactly what was on his mind. But now I'm not so sure." She giggled. "I don't think I've ever heard such a confusen bunch of words that said so little in my entire life."

John thought about it, then laughed with her. "I reckon you're right. That was quite a statement, wasn't it."

"Maybe you ought to be a politician."

"Maybe so."

She took his hand again. "Does this thing that seems so important, and really isn't as important as other things—like Mary Ellen growen up—does it have anythen to do with Sheriff Bridges comen here last week?"

"How'd you know about that?"

"Well, when you lie around in bed all day, and can't see what's goen on, you get pretty good at figuren out the sounds of things. Did you ever notice that Sheriff Bridges' car has sort of a chirping sound in the motor? It sounds like he has a little bird in it."

"I reckon he needs some grease in his water pump."

Olivia smiled, waiting.

"Well," he finally said, "His visit really didn't have anythen to do with it. But somehow the two got mixed up. It made things a little complicated."

"I don't think they're complicated at all," Olivia said with mock seriousness. "It all seems very simple."

They both laughed at that.

"When do I get to hear about it?" she finally asked.

"Oh. Well—pretty soon, I hope."

"John Walton, I love you very much. I think you're a little crazy, but consideren all your other virtues, I reckon I'll just have to overlook that."

John reached across and touched her face. He'd said he would go on enjoying being her husband no matter how the treatments worked out. Now he knew how true that was. He kissed her, then kissed her again to stop her giggling.

A light knock on the door finally put an end to it. Erin was peering in.

"Mama?"

"We're over here, sweetheart."

"What's all the noise? It sounded like you were laughing."

John smiled. "I wouldn't be surprised if you're right about that."

"How come you've got the lights out?"

"We're spoonen."

"Oh." Erin smiled uncertainly and backed out. "Well, everybody's goen to bed. Goodnight."

"Goodnight, dear."

A few minutes later, the round of goodnights went from bedroom to bedroom.

"You gonna stay up till Mary Ellen gets home, Mama?" Jason called.

"Yes, I am."

"Goodnight, Mama."

"Goodnight."

It was a few minutes after eleven before they saw the pair of headlights come bouncing along the road toward the house. Olivia took an anxious breath and squeezed John's hand. "I hope it didn't turn out too badly."

"Why should it have turned out bad at all?"

"You'd better put me back in bed."

John switched on the lights and carried her back. When he returned to the window, G. W. was already headed back home. John wondered if that meant anything—a brief handshake at the door, and then had G. W. bolted for the car?

His heart sank a little when the bedroom door finally opened. The solemn look on Mary Ellen's face had all the earmarks of a disaster.

"Well," Olivia asked hopefully, "how was it?"

Mary Ellen closed the door and glanced from one to the other.

"Didn't you have a good time?" John asked.

She shook her head as if in a trance. "At first, it was just terrible. Worse than I expected. Everybody just stood around staren at everybody else." She smiled faintly. "Then G. W. and I started dancen, and—and it didn't seem so bad." Her smile suddenly became dreamy. "And, Mama, when it was time to go home, I just didn't want it ever to end! Oh, Mama, it was—it was just wonderful."

John grinned and looked quickly at Olivia. There were tears in her eyes and she was holding out her arms for Mary Ellen. "Oh, darlin', I'm so happy!"

Mary Ellen hurried across and they hugged each other. When they separated Mary Ellen's eyes were bright with excitement. "I don't think I ever had so much fun in my life. The music and everythen was just perfect! And Mama, three boys already asked me to go to the next dance!"

"How did G. W. feel about that?"

"I don't think he liked it much. He wanted me to promise never to go dancen with anybody but him."

"Did you promise?"

"I told him I'd think about it." She gave her mother a smug smile and then they both laughed.

John listened silently while the two of them spent another half hour discussing who was at the dance, what each of the girls were wearing, and who they danced with. When Mary Ellen finally said goodnight and floated off to bed, Olivia gave him a concerned look.

"Do you reckon now we're goen to have a dozen boys hangen around the house the way G. W.'s been?"

"Livvy, an hour ago you were scared to death nobody in the world was ever goen to dance with Mary Ellen. Now you're scared to death every boy in the county's fallin in love with her."

She smiled sheepishly. "That's true, isn't it. I reckon we just oughta let things happen the way they happen."

John nodded. "That sounds sensible to me."

XI

John-Boy was not certain how he was going to handle the situation. He wasn't even sure if he had the nerve to go through with it. But he continued walking—past Ike's, past the schoolhouse, and on out toward the Claybournes'. It was cold out, and the ground was beginning to freeze up again. With his collar turned up, he kept his hands deep in his pockets.

It had to be Stuart Lee. John-Boy had gone over it in his mind a hundred times now, and for anybody else to have taken that silver just didn't make any sense. He had ruled out Dewey completely. After working for three generations of Claybournes, Dewey had no reason to begin stealing in his old age. And if Mrs. Claybourne had sold the silver herself, it would be stupid for her to call Sheriff Bridges and accuse John-Boy's father of stealing it. She would have nothing to gain by doing such a thing.

That left only Amelia and Stuart Lee, and John-Boy ruled out Amelia for the same reasons he ruled out her mother. If Amelia took it, she might hope everyone would think John Walton was the thief. But she wouldn't be crazy enough to broadcast it around and risk all the Waltons getting so mad they would do something about it.

So it must be Stuart Lee. From everything John-Boy had heard, Stuart Lee was trying as hard as he could to minimize the whole thing and stop his mother from ruffling people's feathers. Ordinarily this would seem like a virtue, and greatly to Stuart Lee's credit. But in this case John-Boy didn't think so. Stuart Lee must have taken the silver and sold it, and he was trying to stop things from getting out of hand. That was the only answer that seemed logical to John-Boy.

He had made his decision to confront Stuart Lee early in the afternoon. But the hardest part so far had been getting away from the family.

"You mean you're not goen to the amateur contest with us?" Grandpa asked in disbelief.

"I don't think we can afford for all of us to go, Grandpa. And I think Grandma would enjoy seein' it more than anybody."

"No, I'll just stay home with Livvy," Grandma said.

In the end, John-Boy's father insisted that he stay home with Olivia, and it was agreed that John-Boy would stay with him. As quickly as they all left in the truck and his father went upstairs, John-Boy slipped silently away and headed for the Claybournes'.

It was dark now, and John-Boy's first sight of the Claybourne house didn't give him much encouragement. Only one room appeared to be lighted, and that was very dim. Mostly the house looked silent and foreboding. John-Boy slackened his pace as he moved up the long driveway. If Stuart Lee wasn't home, what was he going to do? He couldn't possibly confront Mrs. Claybourne with his suspicions. And what if Stuart Lee was home and flatly denied his accusations? Suddenly the whole idea didn't seem quite so simple as when he first thought of it.

Close to the house now, John-Boy stopped and looked up at the long row of darkened windows above. There was no sound coming from the house. He moved a little closer to the only lighted windows. Then he caught his breath and quickly turned around.

A pair of headlights had flashed across the house. Now a car was coming rapidly up the drive. John-Boy looked around, then stepped behind a large bush and ducked, his heart pounding. My God, what was he doing? If someone saw him here they would probably shoot him for a prowler.

The car's headlights seemed to be shining directly on him for a minute, and then they swept past. John-Boy cautiously raised his head.

It was the yellow roadster—Stuart Lee's car. John-Boy watched him get out and slam the door. Then he was coming around the back of the car, moving quickly toward the house.

"Stuart Lee!"

John-Boy startled himself as much as he frightened Stuart Lee. He moved quickly out of the bushes.

"Oh—it's you, John-Boy. You scared me half to death."

John-Boy smiled, trying to calm his own nerves. "You been out callen on Blanche Weatherby?"

"Well—yes, as a matter of fact I have." He shoved a hand into his pocket and laughed uneasily. "In fact, I've got some good news tonight. Blanche and I are going to be married."

Stuart Lee suddenly frowned—no doubt expecting an explanation of John-Boy's presence. John-Boy quickly decided that the only way he could go through with this was to take the offensive. "That's wonderful news, Stuart Lee. A girl like Blanche Weatherby—I reckon you'll have to make some changes before you bring her here." He glanced up at the house.

"Changes?"

John-Boy smiled. "Oh, I've seen the Weatherbys' place. Everythen neat as a pin. Grass cut just so—must take two or three gardeners to keep it all so perfect."

Stuart Lee looked out at his own lawn. "Yes, well—I've been doing the gardening around here myself. Helps to keep me in shape."

"But who's been doen the cooken? I heard Mrs. Docksteader's been gone for awhile. I sure hope she isn't real sick."

"Mrs. Docksteader went back to Georgia. My mother just hasn't had time to replace her yet."

From Stuart Lee's nervousness, John-Boy guessed that he knew very well what was going on. "Must be a million good cooks looken for jobs these days," John-Boy said. "Shouldn't take too much time to find one."

Stuart Lee nodded, then tried to change the subject. "How's Amelia doing in school?"

"Pretty good. But I think she misses a lot of the friends she had at private school."

"Uh—look, John-Boy, why don't we go inside and—"

Stuart Lee headed for the steps, but John-Boy didn't move. "It's late, Stuart Lee. And I came over to tell you somethen I've been thinken about."

"Well, maybe we could talk in the morning."

"I'd rather talk now. You see, I was readen a book the other night and the author said somethen that seemed real true to me. He said, 'We mortals, men and women, swallow a lot of disappointment between breakfast and dinnertime. Pride helps us; and pride isn't a bad thing when we use it to hide our own hurts. But when pride hurts other people—' " John-Boy broke off, letting the words hang in the silence.

After all his squirming, Stuart Lee suddenly had a look of weary defeat. When he finally spoke his voice was soft. "You know, don't you."

John-Boy nodded. "I know my daddy never stole anythen."

"John-Boy, I—maybe I can explain."

Whatever explanation Stuart Lee might have had was interrupted by the front door opening. Dewey peered out and then shuffled forward. He looked agitated. "Mr. Claybourne—I'm so glad you're back."

"Is something wrong?"

"Yes sir, it's your Mama, Mr. Claybourne. She was getten more and more worked up about those goblets this afternoon and evenen, and—" He glanced nervously at John-Boy, "—and a while ago she went out."

"Where to?"

In his distress, Dewey could hardly get the words out. "Well, sir, she said—she said she was goen over—over to the Walton place. She said she was goen to get those things back no matter what."

"Oh, my God," Stuart Lee groaned.

"I think you'd better do somethen, Mr. Claybourne. When she left here she was awful upset."

"Stuart Lee," John-Boy said, "I think we'd better get on over there."

John heard the knocking on the front door, but paid little attention to it at first. Olivia was sleeping, and he knew John-Boy was somewhere in the house. But after several minutes, and the pounding became more insistent, he went down to the living room.

"John-Boy?" There was no answer.

John swung the door wide, and stiffened. His greeting came from force of habit more than anything. "Mrs. Claybourne."

She marched past him and turned abruptly. "John Walton, I've come for the return of my property."

She was obviously in an emotional state, almost trembling as she glared at him.

John only half closed the door. "Mrs. Claybourne, you've made a mistake, and I think you'd better leave my house."

She shook her head. "This pains me deeply, Mr. Walton. Under the circumstances, I have the greatest sympathy for your wife. But that does not excuse what you have done. Nor am I going to permit you and your friend, Sheriff Bridges, to let this matter rest."

John felt his anger rising. "Mrs. Claybourne, I am not a thief, and I think we'd better end this discussion right now."

She ignored the suggestion, lifting her chin, more determined than ever. "It does not please me to have to say these things, Mr. Walton. I do understand how

hard times are, and how, under your particular circumstances, you might be forced to do something
repellent to you. Nevertheless, I must insist that my
belongings be returned."

The thought of physically grabbing her arm and es-
corting her back to her car occurred to John. But he
quickly dismissed it. He pulled the door open wider.

"Mrs. Claybourne, I want you to leave."

In his fury, John had not heard the car, nor the
two doors slamming outside. But suddenly Stuart Lee
Claybourne and then John-Boy came into the room.
Mrs. Claybourne was equally surprised, but she recovered quickly. "You mustn't be angry, Stuart Lee. I am
only doing what I have to do. Now, Mr. Walton—"

"Mother, wait!"

"I have waited long enough, and I insist—"

Stuart Lee turned sharply to John, paying no attention to his mother's words. He looked tired. "Mr.
Walton," he said hesitantly, "I—I am the one who
took the silver."

John wasn't sure he'd heard correctly. And Stuart
Lee's arrival, he had assumed, was no more than an attempt to calm his mother. "You what?"

"Stuart Lee!" his mother exclaimed, "What are you
saying?"

"Please, Mother." Stuart Lee nodded, affirming his
statement. "Mr. Walton, my mother never understood
about money. My father protected her and didn't
ever want her to worry about anything except being
beautiful and being his wife." He took a deep breath,
forcing himself to go on. "When he died, nobody had
the courage to break the bad news about our finances
to her."

"What bad news?"

"Our money is gone, Mr. Walton." He turned back
to his mother. She had lowered herself shakily into a
chair, apparently in a state of shock.

"Without thinking it out, Mother, I did what father
always did. I tried to protect you. I tried to keep your
life the way it's always been."

"Please don't say any more," she whimpered.

Stuart Lee took another long breath. "I have to, Mama. Our money was all gone several months ago. That's why I started selling off things. They're all gone, Mother. The jewelry, the pewter collection—all the things you thought we stored away in the attic."

"I don't believe that," she said weakly. "You can't be telling the truth, Stuart Lee."

"I am, Mama. There's nothing more to say, except to Mr. Walton." He looked at John. "I'm very ashamed."

John had not moved from the door. The revelations were as shocking to him as they must have been to Mrs. Claybourne. But they still didn't excuse Stuart Lee's letting his mother make those accusations. John suddenly felt angry again. All the grief of the past two weeks could have been avoided if Stuart Lee had had the guts to admit all this from the start.

"I don't think bein' ashamed is good enough, Stuart Lee."

Mrs. Claybourne rose and moved slowly across the room. It seemed to John-Boy that she suddenly looked twenty years older. "The truth is extremely painful, Mr. Walton—and I share the same feelings as my son. My actions have resulted in pain and grief for us all. I most humbly beg your pardon. Please take me home, son."

"Stuart Lee," John said before they could go, "I think you owe us a more public apology. I want you to make sure the sheriff knows exactly what happened."

Stuart Lee moved quickly to help his mother. "I will, Mr. Walton. And I—I'm very sorry."

John watched them move slowly down the steps, and then quietly closed the door. With his hand still on the knob he gazed absently at the floor.

"Well, that's over," John-Boy said softly.

John nodded.

"It's kind of sad, them bein' broke like that."

His father seemed to be only half listening. "Did you get Stuart Lee to confess?" he asked quietly.

"Yes."

His father smiled and moved toward the stairs.

"Daddy?"

He stopped with his hand on the bannister.

"Aren't you goen to tell me what's been troublen you?"

"Yes, I am." He smiled thoughtfully. "I reckon I've got some explainen to do to the whole family. Especially your mother. Can you wait till they all get home?"

"I reckon."

"And thanks, John-Boy. I appreciate what you did. I really do."

John-Boy jumped up from his desk and went quickly to the window when he heard the truck come rattling into the yard. But as quickly as he got to the window the headlights clicked off and he could see nothing in the darkness.

"They're here, Daddy!" He rushed to their bedroom, but only his mother was there. "They're home, Mama. Where's Daddy?"

She was sitting up, smiling, hastily pinning her hair back. "He already went down. Do you think Jason won?"

"I hope so." John-Boy listened for a minute. "I don't know. They're awfully quiet."

She gave him an anxious look. "Well, if he didn't, let's not act too disappointed."

John-Boy moved back toward the door, but his father came bursting in. John-Boy could tell nothing from his expression.

"Well? What happened? John! What're you doen?"

John went directly to the bed and gathered the quilt around Olivia, picking her up. There was a faint smile on his face.

"They're not sayen what happened. They want to

show you. John-Boy, get that other blanket." His father swept past him, his mother holding on tight.

John-Boy got the blanket and followed. When he got down, everyone was in the living room. They were pushing chairs back, clearing an area in the middle of the room. His mother was already on the sofa, with Erin propping pillows behind her.

"What's goen on?" Olivia smiled, "Did you win, Jason?"

"Just hold on, Livvy," Grandpa said, "Wait'll we get settled here."

From the way everyone was trying so hard to keep a straight face, John-Boy suspected that Jason had won the contest. More chairs were brought in from the kitchen, and finally Mary Ellen stepped to the middle of the room.

"All right, now," she smiled, "Comen home, we all decided that Mama and Daddy and John-Boy should see at least part of the show. So Grandpa has very kindly volunteered to fill in as Osgood Tennyson, radio's greatest discoverer of r-a-a-a-a-w talent!" She bowed and gestured grandly to Grandpa. "And here he is now, directly from N-o-o-o-o York City! Mr. Tennyson!"

They all clapped. Grandpa pulled himself to his feet and held up his hands. "Please—no applause. I'm really far too modest to properly play the part of the great Osgood Tennyson—"

"Hmph!" Grandma snorted.

"—However, I'll try. Now then, my friends—and I know you all are my friends—all faithfully listen to my incomparable show each and every Monday night on your favorite radio station. Tonight, as usual, I have assembled a collection of performers on this stage that would put P. T. Barnum to shame—turn Florenz Ziegfeld green with envy. First, I give you one of the most remarkable animal acts I have ever seen on any stage! The Whistler and His Dog!"

Ben jumped up and took the stage. He smiled around at his audience, then snapped his fingers. Yelping and whimpering Jim-Bob scampered into the middle of the room on all fours. Ben had him sit up, shake hands, run after a stick and then play dead.

"Have you ever seen anythen like that in all your lives, ladies and gentlemen?" Grandpa said when the applause ended. "Didn't I warn you it was a remarkable act? That dog is truly brilliant. All he needs is a new master. And next we come to Marvin the Magician, who will astound and mystify you with an exhibition of magic and legerdemain! I give you Marvin the Magician!"

There was applause, but nobody rose. Erin finally jumped up and whispered in Grandpa's ear.

"Oh, I see. Well, ladies and gentlemen, I have just been informed that backstage Marvin the Magician has already performed his most sensational trick. He has disappeared! So we'll move quickly on to our next contestant: Eleanor the Elocutionist. Let's give the little lady a big hand!"

John-Boy glanced at his mother while he clapped. She already had tears in her eyes from laughing.

Elizabeth moved to the middle of the floor, a finger hooked in her mouth. "Mary had a little lamb, its fleece was black as soot. And everywhere that Mary went, on her dress his sooty foot he put!"

"How about that!" Grandpa exclaimed, leading the applause. "Isn't she sensational? And only thirty-five years old! And now, moven right along, we have Jazzbo—no, Jason Wilton—er, Walton—who will be picken and singen his own original composition, the 'Ironing Board Blues'!"

With the applause Jason bowed and placed a chair in the middle of the room. He put his foot up and swung his guitar in place. "I'd like to dedicate this to my grandma, right out there in the audience—who inspired it."

Grandma grinned. She had to rise and take a bow to stop the clapping, and finally Jason played.

John-Boy was surprised at how good he was. The song started quietly, and had a sad, plaintive sound.

Then, as the rhythm picked up John-Boy could almost see Grandma's elbow swinging across the ironing board. If Jason performed that well at the contest, there wasn't much doubt who had won. When he finished, the applause was wild. Ben whistled and stamped his feet, and the others rose for a standing ovation.

"All right," Grandpa said, "All right. You liked it and so did I. It was real good singen and picken. So, despite the splendid talents of all our other contestants, I have no alternative but to award First Prize to Jazzbo Wilton—or whatever his name may be."

They applauded wildly again. From behind a chair Grandpa brought out a shiny new guitar and handed it to Olivia.

"Jason! You really won!" she cried, "Oh, it's beautiful!"

"Yes, I did, Mama. It's a humdinger, isn't it?"

John-Boy was surprised by the quality of the instrument. After what he'd seen of Mr. Tennyson's advance man, he half expected the guitar to be a toy.

Olivia sighed heavily and looked around. "I'm so pleased for you, Jason. And thank you all for the show. It was almost as good as bein' there."

"I think Grandpa was better," Jim-Bob smiled.

"He oughta be on the radio," Elizabeth said.

"Don't tell him things like that," Grandma muttered, "He's conceited enough already."

Grandpa laughed. "Well, bein' married two thousand years to the most elegant lady in Jefferson County has finally gone to my head, I reckon."

Grandma started to get up. "Well, I reckon we could use a pot of coffee around here."

"Wait a minute, Mama."

The request came from his father, and John-Boy looked quickly at him. He was sitting in the big chair next to Olivia, holding her hand now.

"I reckon with everybody here, this is a good time for me to do some explainen about some things." He smiled and glanced at John-Boy. "First off, I should tell you that Mrs. Claybourne and Stuart Lee came over to the house tonight."

"They came *here*?" They all gaped at him. Olivia looked around, puzzled.

"That's right," John went on, "And Stuart Lee confessed that he was the one who took all the Claybournes' silver."

"Well, I declare!" Grandma exclaimed.

"But why would Stuart Lee take it, Daddy?"

"Well, it seems like the Claybournes have been sufferen from the Depression as much as anybody else around Walton's Mountain. So to keep his mother from known how broke they were, he pawned the family silver."

"That's terrible! Did he apologize, Daddy?"

"Yes, he did. They both did."

"What're you all talken about?" Olivia asked.

"Well, I'll explain later, Livvy. But the Claybournes' silver is not the main thing I wanted to tell you about." He smiled at Olivia and went on, "A couple of weeks ago when Sheriff Bridges came around asken if I took that silver, I reckon you all thought I acted pretty strange tellen him it was none of his business where I'd been that day. Well, I did that partly on the principle that it really wasn't any of his business. But I was also feelen a little guilty about somethen." He studied the floor for a minute. "You remember, that was just after your Mama got sick. And I reckon we were about as broke as we've ever been. I wanted to get your mama somethen. And we had to have tires for the truck. Anyhow, I did somethen I didn't guess I'd ever do in my life. I took my wedden ring down to Charlottesville and pawned it."

His mother was holding his father's hand, and John-Boy saw her glance down at it. But she didn't appear to be surprised by the absence of the ring.

"When I handed that ring over to the man in the pawnshop, I thought it was the best thing to do. I thought more than anythen, Livvy needed some cheeren up, and some nice present would do it for her. But as quick as I headed home I started feelen different about it." He gave a short laugh and shook his head. "I reckon I felt like I'd sold my soul to the devil or somethen. And the more I thought about it the worse it got. And that's about when Ep came around asken where I'd been."

Elizabeth looked stricken. "Does that mean you and Mama aren't married anymore?"

Olivia smiled. "It doesn't mean that at all, darling. It means we love each other so much it doesn't make any difference whether Daddy wears his ring or not."

John smiled at her. "Well, your mother's bein' very brave about all this. But that ring ain't gonna stay in that pawnshop much longer."

Olivia gave him an anxious look. "Do you think you can get it back, John?"

"I think I can get it back first thing Monday mornen."

"But—"

John's smile broadened. "I was down at Ike's today, and George Halverson called while I was there. You know that bridge he's supposed to build? Well, now they want it built as fast as possible. And George wants us to start deliveren those timbers as quick as we can get 'em cut and hauled over there."

Grandpa slapped his knee and grinned. "And we got most of 'em cut already!"

"That's right, Pa. And George is payen on delivery. So I figure we'll be waiten for him with a load first thing Monday mornen."

John-Boy felt a wave of relief. They had been trimming those logs and stacking them in the barn for almost three weeks now. And with delivery not scheduled until May or June, it had all seemed foolish to him.

"Well, now I do think I'm goen to make some coffee," Grandma smiled. "Maybe I'll make two pots. And it just so happens that I've got a little surprise hidden up in the cupboard."

Grandma's surprise turned out to be an angel food

cake with the words, *Congratulations, Jason,* written
on it in pink icing. While they ate it, Mary Ellen told
them more about the talent contest. The other contestants, she said, were really not as good as the imita-
tions Ben, Jim-Bob, and Elizabeth did. If Jason hadn't
won the first prize the audience probably would have
torn the theater down.

When they were finished with the cake, John
gathered the quilt around Olivia, ready to take her
upstairs. "John," she said, "can I try somethen?"

Everyone was picking up dishes, carrying them to
the kitchen—but they stopped now.

"Try what, Livvy?"

"I'd like to try and stand up—on my own."

John-Boy saw the shadow of doubt cross his father's face.

"You really think you ought to?"

"Well, everybody else gave a performance tonight.
I'd like to have a turn, too. I think I can do it, John."

"Maybe you ought to wait till tomorrow mornen,
Mama," John-Boy suggested.

She laughed, trying to dismiss their concern. "Tomorrow is Easter and I'm goen to walk. All I want to
do tonight is stand up." She held out her hand.
"Please, John? Can I try?"

John-Boy guessed a pin would have made a very
loud noise if it dropped right then. It had been more
than a week since anyone had mentioned her vow to
walk to Easter sunrise services. And through the past
few days everyone had almost been holding his
breath, hoping she wouldn't mention it either.

She had made efforts to stand during the week.
John and Grandpa had each held an arm, and with
their help she had been able to half support herself
and move a couple of steps. But no one had any hope
of her walking for a long time. And from the
lighthearted manner in which she mentioned the sunrise services, neither did she.

John-Boy almost wished Jason hadn't won the contest, or that they all hadn't had such a good time re-

creating it for her. She seemed to want desperately to make some contribution to the evening.

John-Boy's father seemed to share his uneasiness. But he finally smiled and took both her hands.

"Now, just take it slow and easy, Livvy." He grasped her by the elbows and she gripped his forearms as she came shakily to her feet.

She was up. She stood for a minute and then released her grip on his arms.

"I'm all right, John. Just let me get balanced, then let me go."

She seemed to be steady, and John eased away, holding only one hand now.

"That's good, Mama," Erin said. "That's marvelous!"

She swayed almost imperceptibly. But she was supporting herself, using John's hand only for balance.

"I think that's enough, Livvy."

"No. Just for a second, let go of my hand."

John let go, but he stood ready, and for a minute she was standing alone, her mouth open, scarcely breathing.

Because of her long nightgown, John-Boy couldn't tell if her legs were quivering. But she appeared to be steady and in control.

"You did it, Mama!" Jason said.

"Well, I declare!" Grandma sighed.

A smile came to John's face as he watched her. Then he stepped forward.

She waved him away. "No. Just a minute."

John-Boy knew what was coming. She was biting her lip, a determined look on her face, and from his angle at the side, he could see her leaning forward, preparing to take a step. Every muscle in her body was straining with the tension.

Then it happened.

"Mama!" John-Boy shouted.

He had begun to move toward her, but he was too late. Even his father's quick grab for her arm was not enough to stop the fall. For an instant it seemed as if her effort was successful. She had taken the step and she was still upright. She might have been someone casually heading for the kitchen. In the next instant, her legs were gone from beneath her.

She hit the low table in front of the sofa, grasping at it, trying to break the fall. Then she was on the floor.

"Livvy!"

"Good Lord!" Grandma cried.

They all rushed forward. John-Boy got her other arm, and his father quickly got a hand under her shoulders.

"Are you all right, Livvy?"

She was grimacing, trying to straighten her useless legs. "I think so. I—"

With one movement, John scooped her up and put her on the sofa. John-Boy got a pillow behind her.

It had all happened so suddenly—she was down, and then back on the sofa so quickly—that even Olivia seemed stunned and speechless. John looked anxiously at her.

"You sure you're all right? Did you hurt your legs?"

"I—" She shook her head and brought a hand to her face, touching her forehead.

At first John-Boy thought she was going to laugh. She seemed confused for a moment and a faint smile came to her lips. But then her face contorted and she covered it with both hands. She turned away, and a torrent of sobbing and tears shook her whole body.

"Does it hurt, Livvy? What's the matter?"

She shook her head, unable to control the crying.

"Mama, you stood up," Erin said, "For a minute you stood up all by yourself. That's a lot more than you could do a week ago."

John sat down and gently pulled her head to his shoulder. "Livvy, you're doen fine. A lot better than anybody ever expected you to."

"That's right," Grandpa said. "There's no reason you have to walk by Easter."

John-Boy felt his own throat clogged with tears and disappointment. Along with everyone else in the room, he knew she was not crying from pain. The tears were for the three weeks of struggle and agony, and the desperate hope that tonight she would have something to show for it. John-Boy had never before seen such rigid determination on anyone's face as when she tried to take that step.

She finally took her hands away. She took a deep, recovering breath and shook her head. "This is silly, isn't it." She forced a smile. "Has anybody got a handkerchief?"

Grandpa found one in his pocket. She dried her eyes and blew her nose. "I'm sorry. I really thought I could do it. I've been practicen all week—putten my feet on the floor and putten some weight on them. I was goen to surprise you all and take a step."

"You did fine, Livvy. You surprised us enough just standen up by yourself."

She shook her head. "But I felt so good today. Even the pains were almost gone. I just—I just thought for sure I could take a step."

"You will, Livvy," Grandma said. "It'll come soon enough."

"Mama," John-Boy said, "maybe you've just been tryen too hard. Sometimes when you're tryen to learn somethen new and your mind wants your body to do certain things, the more you think about it, the more stubborn your body gets. You said you feel good, and there isn't much pain anymore. Maybe you're just concentraten too hard."

"That might be, Livvy," Grandpa nodded.

"I remember when Daddy was teachen me to swim," John-Boy went on. "At first I tensed up and strained so hard to keep my mind on all the things he said, and I almost drowned. Then, when I relaxed more and stopped thinken so much, it came easy."

John-Boy wasn't sure if she was even listening to him. She suddenly looked weak and tired and defeated. She smiled and looked wearily at John.

"I think I'd better go back up to bed."

John nodded and started gathering the quilt around her.

"It might be somethen to think about, Mama," John-Boy suggested.

She gave him a sad smile. "John-Boy, I'm so tired of thinken about it, I'm not sure I even want to try anymore."

"Goodnight, Mama."

"Goodnight everybody. And thank you all for a nice evenen."

She clung to John's neck and her eyes were closed as they went up the stairs.

XII

It was a night John-Boy would remember for the rest of his life. Three weeks earlier when his father had sat down in the kitchen and told everyone their mother had polio, Grandpa had remarked that God worked in mysterious ways. But he hadn't finished the quote: "God works in mysterious ways, *His miracles to perform.*" John-Boy guessed that the closest thing to a miracle he would ever see came on that Easter Eve.

After Olivia had gone to bed there was little more to say. They cleaned up the dishes from the cake, and as Elizabeth climbed the stairs her glum comment seemed to sum up the evening.

"The crocuses aren't bloomin either," she muttered.

John-Boy couldn't sleep. For an hour he sat at his desk with his chin resting in his hand and stared vacantly at his notebook. He couldn't write anything, either. The question of the Claybournes' silver had been cleared up, and Jason had won the amateur contest. But these things seemed inconsequential now. Most of his thoughts revolved around statements that had been made by Dr. Vance: Mrs. Walton may think she has feeling in her legs, but this could be in her imagination. Most polio patients do show some improvement. But it is always limited by the extent of the nerve damage. Her recovery could stop at any time. Your wife is no different from thousands of others, Mr. Walton. They all have hopes and are confident of recovery. They are all disappointed.

Even Dr. Miller had told her that life in a wheelchair wasn't so bad. She should accept the fact that there were other possibilities.

John-Boy finally tossed his pencil down and moved to the window. Behind him the house was silent, and he could see the broad shadow of Walton's Mountain dominating the horizon. Tomorrow morning at sunrise the entire church congregation would be up there on its slopes celebrating the dawn of Easter. It would be the first time his mother and the rest of the family wouldn't be with them.

He remembered the previous Easter. His mother had worn a new white dress that Grandma had made and surprised her with. And she had a new white hat with yellow flowers all around the brim. John-Boy guessed his mother had never looked so beautiful as she did that day.

And even his father had attended the service. He had marched proudly up the hill with Olivia on his arm, and then bellowed out the hymns so loud they echoed for miles through the mountains. "Welcome happy morning! Age to age shall say. Hell today is vanquished, heaven is won today!"

That day it really seemed that heaven had won.

John-Boy finally buried himself in the bed. He stretched himself out and then pulled the comforter high around his ears as if to shut out the world. Silently, as he gazed off at the dark window, he said The Lord's Prayer to himself, and then he went to sleep.

At first he thought it was a dream. Flashes of light were all around him and a soft rumbling faded slowly into the distance. John-Boy only half awakened. Another flash of lightning illuminated the window and at the same moment raindrops splattered across the window pane. It was a storm, but it was more like those of summer or spring rather than the harsh thrashings they had through the winter.

John-Boy gazed at the window for a minute and then suddenly realized what had awakened him. It was not the lightning or thunder, but Elizabeth's whimpering cries from the next room. Just as Erin had been before her, Elizabeth was scared to death of thunder. John-Boy lay silently in the bed for a minute, half expecting to hear his mother's footsteps hurrying to comfort her. But then the realization of his mother's condition struck him.

He quickly swung his feet from under the covers and groped for the lamp switch. When he got it turned on, he moved toward the door, rubbing his eyes, still not certain if he was completely awake.

"It's Elizabeth, John-Boy."

"Yes, I know, Mama, I'll—"

The light was on in the hallway. There had been no thunder or lightning for several minutes now, and Elizabeth's crying seemed to have stopped. But none of these facts were registering in John-Boy's mind. Instead, he stood frozen in the doorway, gaping down the hall. Was he still asleep, dreaming?

Standing just outside her bedroom, her hand still on the light switch, was his mother. She was swaying a little, and her eyes had the faraway look of someone only half awake. But she was not going to fall.

"Mama?"

"She's cryen because of the thunder, John-Boy."

John-Boy stood petrified as he watched her come toward him. She took one step, then another, supporting herself with a hand against the wall. Then she stopped.

For a minute they gazed at each other; John-Boy's heart pounding, almost bursting inside his chest— Olivia blinking, her mouth opening and closing.

"John-Boy," she finally breathed, and the realization and certainty that she, too, was not dreaming suddenly hit her. "John-Boy, I'm walking! Oh, dear Lord!"

John-Boy could hardly remember what happened next. It seemed like fireworks were going off inside him, and he was rushing toward her. She reached for him with both arms and they hugged each other. And then his father was there. Then his father and mother were hugging each other, and John-Boy was shouting at the top of his lungs. Half a minute later Grandpa and Grandma, and five bleary-eyed children were coming from doorways, gaping at them.

I guess it was about the biggest celebration we ever had, John-Boy wrote later in his notebook. *I don't know what time it was—nobody looked at the clock. But none of us went back to bed.*

That she had walked from her bed across the room to the door even before John-Boy saw her seemed incredible. But before that night was over she repeated the performance. Part of the way she used the bed for support. Then, after steadying herself for a minute, she wobbled her way across to the support of the doorway. There, she clung to the door frame and smiled happily at all of them.

"What were you thinken about, Mama?" Elizabeth asked. "Didn't you even know you were walken?"

"I was just thinken about you, darlin. And I guess I was half asleep. And John-Boy, I reckon you were right. I've just been concentraten too hard and wanten it too much. But if I just forget my legs and think about getten somewhere—" She grinned, too filled with joy to go on.

"Well, hallelujah!" Grandma must have said twenty times that night.

We did go to the sunrise services that day. The thunder showers had left the pine boughs and new spring leaves fresh and fragrant. Daddy helped Mama up the slope, and their beaming smiles were about twice as bright as the sun when it finally came over the shoulder of Walton's Mountain.

Dr. Vance once said he didn't believe in miracles, and Grandma expressed pity for him. Whether what happened that night was a miracle or not doesn't really seem important. Dr. Vance was doing the best he could, and so was Mama. For that, I'm inclined to think that God was helping them both.

What seemed as miraculous as anything was the fact that Elizabeth and Jim-Bob's crocuses were in full bloom when we arrived home.

Mama was speechless. She stood by the truck admiring them for a long time. When she finally took Elizabeth and Jim-Bob into her arms, her happy tears were the most joyful present any of us could possibly have for Easter.

ABOUT THE AUTHOR

ROBERT WEVERKA was born in Los Angeles and educated at the University of Southern California, where he majored in economics. His novels include: *Griff, Search, The Sting, Moonrock, The Widowed Master, One Minute to Eternity, Apple's Way, I Love My Wife* and his stories of the Walton family; *The Waltons, The Waltons: Trouble on the Mountain* and *The Waltons: The Easter Story*. He and his family currently live in Idylwild, California.